FONTHILL

A Comedy

Books by Aubrey Menen

Fiction

THE PREVALENCE OF WITCHES

THE STUMBLING STONE

THE BACKWARD BRIDE

THE DUKE OF GALLODORO

THE RAMAYANA

THE ABODE OF LOVE

THE FIG TREE

SHELA

A CONSPIRACY OF WOMEN

FONTHILL

Non-fiction

DEAD MAN IN A SILVER MARKET

ROME FOR OURSELVES

INDIA

(with photographs by Roloff Beny)

SPEAKING THE LANGUAGE LIKE A NATIVE

CITIES IN THE SAND

UPON THIS ROCK

THE NEW MYSTICS

(with photographs by Graham Hall)

FONTHILL

A Comedy

by

AUBREY MENEN

HAMISH HAMILTON
LONDON

First published in Great Britain, 1975
by Hamish Hamilton Ltd
90 Great Russell Street London WC1

Copyright © 1974 by Aubrey Menen

SBN 241 89177 9

Printed in Great Britain by
Northumberland Press Ltd,
Gateshead

Contents

NOTE

William Beckford

(1760-1844)

It is not generally known that part of Fonthill is still standing, though in a dilapidated state. The grounds, however,
have reached that peak of natural beauty at which Beckford
aimed. They are private property, but they may be visited
by persons declaring their interest in the author of *Vathek*.

It was while walking in these grounds that this novel began
to take shape in my mind. During the writing of it (1973) a
standing silver cup collected by Beckford was sold at a London
auction for £40,000; shortly after, Cozens' sketchbooks were
sold for £120,000.

PART ONE

Private View

THE summer of 1822 was hot, but the ladies and gentlemen rolling along in their carriages to the Private View felt delicious cold shudders, first when they caught sight of the celebrated tower of the so-called Abbey, again when they drove past the high wall that surrounded it. The owner of Fonthill had said that he had built the wall to keep out fox hunters: a thin excuse, for what gentleman would want to keep out the hunt? Everyone knew it had been built to hide the nameless vices that went on behind it.

The vices were not really nameless, except in the newspapers which had made such a play of the scandal that had surrounded Beckford, but that was forty years ago. Nowadays women named it in their drawing rooms over a dish of tea, men named it at the tops of their voices in their clubs: 'sodomy', and Beckford would have hanged for it if he had not been the richest man in England.

But God was just. Beckford was rich no longer. The Abbey at which he had laboured a quarter of a century to build was up for sale, with all its contents. For twenty years no decent person in English society had set foot in it. It had been a magnificent display of the moral rectitude of the nation. Not even Byron had gone. William Beckford had eaten his meals alone, off the gold plate which everybody hoped to see, served (it was said) by twenty menials, no doubt naked.

The first carriages drew up at the iron gates. There was a

great deal of tittering when it was seen that the gates were emblazoned with a coat of arms to which Beckford had no right whatsoever. One gentleman leaned his chin on the knob of his cane and said, 'He claimed to be descended from the barons who signed the Magna Carta. When Lancaster Herald asked him which baron, what do you think he replied? He said, "All of them".'

It was disappointing to have the gates opened by a country bumpkin who greeted them surlily enough, in the thick Wiltshire accent of those parts. Each one of the viewers had paid the outrageous sum of a guinea for a catalogue, and good Mr. Christie, the auctioneer, had been profuse in his apologies for the imposition. For that round sum they expected at least turbans and salaams at the gate. Was not the owner, among his other absurdities, fond of being called the Caliph?

But there, at the end of the drive, was Fonthill Abbey. The ladies in the first carriage cast an intense gaze upon it. 'Gothic,' said one of them. 'Romantic,' said another, for that was the thing to say. 'It makes me dream,' said a third, 'of I know not what.'

'It makes me dream of the day that the tower fell down,' said the gentleman with the cane. 'Beckford had run it up with cement and lath and plaster, d'you know, and one stormy night down it all came. Not, unfortunately, on top of Beckford. But I see he's built another one.'

They came to the west entrance and got down from their carriages. It was made of two great wooden doors set in a pointed arch, and each forty feet high. The visitors hesitated, for there was no knocker and no bellpull.

'Open, Sesame,' said the lady who had dreamed of she knew not what. She had been reading the French translation of *The Arabian Nights* in preparation for her visit.

The door creaked; it groaned; it slowly opened, and there

pushing it was a three-foot dwarf of astonishing ugliness. The ladies clapped their hands with delight. With the door half-open the dwarf gazed at the visitors malevolently. He craned his short neck and surveyed the carriages which were waiting in a line behind. He said something obscene in French. The lady who had read *The Arabian Nights* had read them in Galland's translation which is heroically clean. She smiled brightly, nodded, and said, 'We have come to see the Abbey, my dear little man.'

The dwarf stiffened.

'I am the Count Pierre Colas di Grailly,' he said. 'Who the devil are you?'

It was Mr. Christie, the auctioneer, who saved the situation. His spare figure loomed behind the dwarf, his hands clasped together at his chest. Bowing, he greeted these first of the four visitors by their names and titles, for they were all among his clients. He pushed the door wider open, while Count Pierre Colas di Grailly stumped off into the shadows, growling like a dog.

'I do, do apologize,' said Mr. Christie, clasping his hands again, 'for your reception. You see, Mr. Beckford always likes the count to open the door because it seems bigger than it really is. It's pretty big at that. Forty feet. Every inch of forty feet high. A magnificent entrance to the most splendid house in all England.'

None of the four visitors heard him. They were staring in astonishment at the scene before them.

'The Great Western Hall,' said Mr. Christie in the hushed tones of a verger.

The first group of visitors stared at the cavernous place, their eyes slowly adjusting to the gloom. The floor was a Joseph's Coat of glowing colour from the light that came through the stained glass of the tall, pointed windows. They craned their necks to look at the coffered roof.

'Seventy feet above the floor,' whispered Mr. Christie.

A hundred bosses studded the roof, each painted with armorial bearings. A visitor said in a low voice, 'I don't recognize any of the coats of arms,' and another answered, 'Beckford probably made them up.'

Mr. Christie drew aside a red curtain to reveal a niche with a life-sized statue.

'Mr. Beckford's father,' said Mr. Christie. 'He left *our* Mr. Beckford one million pounds and an income of one hundred thousand pounds a year, which made him, if I may quote Lord Byron, "England's wealthiest son!"'

The visitors looked and whispered.

'Where did it all come from?'

'Jamaica.'

'Sugar.'

'Slaves.'

'Shameful.'

'This way, if you please,' said Mr. Christie, raising his voice a little in reproof.

The party moved to the middle of the hall. Before them stretched a perspective of other halls lit sparsely with candles in silver candelabra, except at the far end. Here a vast painted oriel window blazed with the September sun.

'The window is three hundred feet away,' said Mr. Christie. 'As long as many cathedrals. Please follow me to the Great Octagon.'

They moved forward. They came to an eight-sided space. They looked up, their mouths open.

Eight enormous arches surrounded them. 'Each arch is eighty feet high,' said Mr. Christie. Four of the arches were hung with immense blue curtains, four with scarlet. Above soared the famous tower with its lantern. Gothic vaulting sprang from immense pillars. This time there were no comments. Silently the little group marvelled at what a hundred thousand pounds a year could do.

'Before you,' said Mr. Christie with a wave of his hand, 'is King Edward's Gallery. King Edward the First was a distant ancestor of the Beckfords.'

A man said, 'As well as all the Magna Carta barons,' but a woman said, 'Hush, my lord. It is all so beautiful.'

A crimson carpet ran down the gallery to a shrine under the oriel window, so far away that details could be barely discerned. In the middle of the gallery stood a table of marble and inlay. All walked towards it. A cup of gold, surrounded with figures of the same metal, stood on it.

'The Cellini "Nautilus",' said Mr. Christie. 'The most precious of a hundred similar *objets d'art* that Mr. Beckford has collected from all over the world.'

Pictures hung upon the walls between curtained windows, but the gloom was too much for them to be seen.

'As you will observe from the catalogue,' said Mr. Christie, 'Mr. Beckford's collection of pictures includes. . . .' He cleared his throat. In an auctioneer's monotone he said, 'Raphael, Murillo, Claude.'

'Claude! Claude!' whispered a woman, hearing the fashionable name.

'Holbein, Dürer, Van Dyck,' continued Mr. Christie, 'Bellini, Van Eyck and others too numerous to mention, to say nothing of six hundred priceless manuscripts and six thousand books, dozens of which are incunabula.'

'What's that, my lord?' whispered a woman.

'What's what?' said the man.

'Incu—something.'

'God knows. Books about black magic, I shouldn't wonder. He practises it.'

The listening group gave a delightful shudder.

'And all of this comes under the hammer, eh?' said a man at the back of the little group.

'I shall have the historic privilege,' said Mr. Christie primly, 'of offering these treasures to the discerning, including the Abbey with outbuildings and pleasure grounds, at my auction rooms on the seventeenth of this month, at noon precisely.'

The group moved towards the oriel window. They mounted a step to a sort of sanctuary and then stood before the shrine itself. Thirty-six candles, dimmed a little by the light from the great window, shone on a statue of St. Anthony of Padua. The saint held a child in his arms.

A visitor in a heavily laced coat bent towards the ear of another man.

'At last—a *boy*,' he said, grinning. The other man began a guffaw but, seeing the ladies, instantly repressed it.

Mr. Christie, his duties finished, looked curiously at the man who had asked about the auction. In the bright light at this end of the gallery, Christie could see that the man was dressed in a shabby coat, the collar of which was black with grease from his long hair that clearly had not been washed for months. The man was scratching under his dirty stock. His breeches were stained and flapped at one knee for lack of a buckle. His stockings were wrinkled, his shoes filthy.

Mr. Christie looked more closely at this spectacularly grubby man, outstanding among the other visitors, who had dressed for the occasion.

Christie frowned. The man moved, and a beam of sunlight lit up his face.

Christie instantly straightened. He walked over to the man. Mr. Christie bowed his deepest bow.

'Mr. Farquhar,' he said, 'I did not expect to be honoured by your presence so early.'

John Farquhar sat in his vast drawing room in Portman Square and listened to a thunderous knocking on his front door. It was a footman's knock. Farquhar went to the bay window to examine the visitor's carriage. He could see it, but dimly. There was too much dirt on the windowpane to make out who sat in it—somebody of importance, it would seem, for the knocking was resumed even more loudly, and in London one judged social position by the vigour with which a footman hammered on the door.

Farquhar passed a grubby hand across the windowpane and, achieving nothing, shrugged and turned back to the drawing room. He looked around it with satisfaction. Big as it was, a side chapel of Fonthill Abbey could have swallowed it, but in its way, it was just as famous among the gossips. Nobody had been in Fonthill, until the Private View, for a quarter of a century, except Admiral Lord Nelson, but Lord Nelson had his own tastes: did he not paint his face? Nobody at all had ever set foot in this drawing room except Farquhar himself: not even the old woman who was his only servant. That, thought Farquhar, was not because he was suspected of immorality; it was not because of anything, except that he was so rich he could do as he damned well pleased. Like dukes; like the king; like Napoleon before his recent misfortune at Waterloo. Farquhar had always wanted to be like that since he was a poor boy in an Aberdeen slum.

He heard the front door squeak open on its rusty hinges and a footman's voice. He heard his old servant shuffling through the hall and watched a card being thrust under the door. Painfully and slowly, the old man bent and picked it up. It read 'William Beckford; Fonthill Abbey, Wiltshire'; over the name hovered an engraved coronet, in the Continental fashion.

A knot twisted in Farquhar's stomach, as it always did when a rich man's name came his way. But as he studied the card and the black-rimmed fingers that held it, the knot went away. Beckford, he reflected, was rich no longer. Fonthill was for sale. Farquhar sold nothing. He only bought. So far from having to sell his house, he owned most of the square in which it stood.

'Ask Mr. Beckford to come in,' he said through the door. He waited while, to judge from the sounds, this had been done and his guest had been seated in the hall. Then he waited still further.

William Beckford sat in the hall in a great carved chair. He looked at a fellow chair opposite and reflected that if the chair he sat on was as dirty as that one, he had ruined his breeches. He looked around the walls with their peeling paper; he squinted at two pictures, which he dismissed as being in the worst of taste. He listened to the ticking of a grandfather clock and felt his temper rise, tick by tick. He would explode in all his terrible wrath, he decided, when the clock struck the quarter-to.

Then he reflected that his terrible wrath (with the annihilating glare, the famous annihilating glare he had inherited from his father) wouldn't do at all. He was taking the first step in a business which, should he succeed in it, would let him laugh in the face of the world. He must be patient; he must be calm; he must play at being Commander of the Faithful. *That* always helped keep his temper, so there, in the cobwebbed-hung hall in Portman Square (on the corner, to be precise, of the square and Upper Baker Street), he set about doing it.

He fished in a pocket and brought out a pair of dark spectacles, very small in the lenses. He put them on. He had not taken off his tall hat—Farquhar was a commoner, and one did not remove one's hat in the houses of such men. He tilted its curved brim over his face.

He was now the Caliph al-Vathek Bi'llah, son of the Caliph al-Mu'tasim Bi'llah—and grandson of Haroun al-Rashid. He was in Baghdad, and incognito. He had expressed a desire to visit the mysterious house at the angle of the Street of the Bakers and the Square of the Public Porters, for there, he had been told, was a room into which no one but its owner had ever been. Some said it was crammed to the ceiling with caskets of jewels, precious silks from Cathay and India and costly goblets so cunningly wrought that they seemed to be the work of genies. Others said this was not so but that it contained the instruments and symbols, the incense, the powder and the musical instruments which enabled their owner to conjure spirits. This was the opinion of the Grand Vizier (Brown, Beckford's footman, had said the look of the place gave him, with all due respects, the creeps). Vathek had given him one glance, that terrible glance, and the Vizier had touched his master's gold-embroidered sandals and said, 'Commander of the Faithful, to hear is to obey,' and forthwith led him to this place.

Thus William Beckford, sixty-two years old and nearly bankrupt, dreamed the dreams of his boyhood and was happy, for he was a man who devoutly wished he had never been anything more than a boy.

It is the wish of many men, but Beckford once had been rich enough to make it come true. Fonthill was his sand castle, the biggest any boy had ever built.

A cough and a murmured 'Mr. Beckford?' awoke him. He took off his dark glasses. He tilted back his hat. He was instantly, bitterly, awake. The sand castle, he remembered, was soon to be scattered.

He eyed the shabby man before him. The clothes he had expected, but not the wrinkled face, the broad nose and the matted hair low on the forehead. Boylike, Beckford gave everybody he met a nickname, quickly, so that his first impression, wrong as it may turn out to be, always remained. New boys were thus labelled at school.

'"Mr. Monkey,"' he thought, 'but no, "Mr. Filthyman" is better.' He got out of the chair.

'Mr. Farquhar?'

Mr. Filthyman bowed.

'Mr. Farquhar,' Beckford went on, 'I trust you will forgive this intrusion. Mr. Christie told me you have visited Fonthill and....'

'And,' said Farquhar, 'you have returned the visit. No words of mine can express the honour I feel.'

Beckford noticed that the voice was unpolished, the accent provincial. But he also noticed with what skill Farquhar had managed to put them on an equal footing. He had made no apologies for the deplorable state of his home.

Farquhar extended his grimy hand. Beckford removed his hat and extended his own slender and—so people and friends said—his beautiful hand.

Farquhar studied his guest and was surprised. There were no signs of the debaucheries which went on behind the wall. There were even few signs of age. The shock of hair, swept back in the manner of the Romantics, was greying, it was true. But the bold forehead was smooth and joined without a furrow the bold, straight nose; A Classical nose, thought Farquhar, if it could be pushed back a little. The lips were full but innocent, like a young boy's. The eyes were young too, but neither innocent nor experienced. They were the eyes, Farquhar decided, of an adolescent, sad with a newfound knowledge. There was a gentle stoop of the head, as though its owner were bending to look at something beautiful and precious. Farquhar had fallen in love with Fonthill. Now he had a strange feeling of affection towards the man who had built it.

'Filthyman has kind eyes,' thought Beckford. 'But so have monkeys.'

'Yes,' said Farquhar, 'I have had the great experience of seeing Fonthill. But I hope you will believe that when I had recovered my breath, I realized what a melancholy thing it must be for you to part with it.'

'And I hope you will believe me, Mr. Farquhar, that it is nothing of the sort. I have spent twenty years of my life building and furnishing that place, and it is still far from right.'

'I think it was Michelangelo,' said Farquhar, 'who said that a masterpiece is something in which its creator has never realized quite what he set out to do.'

'It was Leonardo da Vinci,' said Beckford. 'Michelangelo had the gift of always blaming his imperfections on somebody else.'

Farquhar moved his hands deprecatingly. 'I am not as well read as I sometimes appear.'

'Alas!' said Beckford. 'I *am*. Another waste of spirit. As it states in Christie's ill-printed and erroneous catalogue—does the man know *no* history?—I have six thousand books in my library and I have read them all. But you, now, are a collector, or so Christie gave me to understand and....'

'I buy things at Christie's auction sales,' said Farquhar. 'The trouble with me is that when I have bought them, I never know what to do with them.'

'While I,' said Beckford, 'spend my time fiddling with them like a woman changing about her ribbons.'

'He has,' thought Farquhar, 'all the appeal of a youth saying to some elder, "But tell me what to *do*!" He must,' thought Farquhar, 'have been a beautiful boy.' He felt a strong desire to keep this man in his company.

'Perhaps you would care to see what I do with *my* ribbons,' he said and opened the door which he had closed behind him. 'Come this way, sir.'

Beckford raised his eyebrows.

'Willingly, sir,' he said. 'Mr. Christie tells me it is a privilege you accord to very few visitors.'

'None,' said Farquhar. 'But then my visitors have never before included Mr. Beckford of Fonthill Abbey.'

(*'No door is closed to the Commander of the Faithful,' said the merchant from Aleppo, bowing to the ground, and he inserted a golden key into a massy lock of the same precious metal.*)

Hearing these words in his mind, Beckford stepped into the room.

The room was hot. A huge fire of logs burned at one end in a grate with an elaborate marble surround, buried for half of its height in logs ready for burning.

Farquhar said, 'I hope it is not too warm for you?'

'Fonthill,' began Beckford, and was about to tell his host that the principal drawback of living there was that it could never be heated properly. Wyatt, his architect, had dismissed the matter with a quip: 'Have you ever been in a warm cathedral?' But Beckford remembered his mission and held his peace. He loosened his stock and looked around the room.

It was crammed with tables, cabinets, vases, statues and pictures. All was in disorder. Chinese vases cluttered a Louis Seize table, as many as could be put on its marble top. A crowd of statuettes occupied another, some with their back to the room. A superb cabinet of ebony inlay had a confusion of lacquer boxes on top of it. An embroidered cape hung on one shoulder of a suit of armour. Oriental rugs lay in piles. A stuffed bird perched on a heap of painted plates. A great golden ewer stood in a golden bowl heaped with medallions. Dust was everywhere. In the middle of the room straight-backed chairs, which Beckford remembered having seen in the palace of the Borghese in Rome, stood around a low table set with semi-precious stones such as the Moguls used. It was as though the treasures of many mansions had been hastily gathered in one place under the threat of an invading army.

'Pray be seated, Mr. Beckford,' said Farquhar, but Beckford, fascinated by the piles of desirable objects, ignored him. He went to a cabinet with two small doors.

'Permit me,' he said. Farquhar nodded. Beckford opened the doors. The cabinets at Fonthill were his joy. Within them he kept his most beautiful things—cups of jade, statuettes of gold and silver, great jewelled morses from the robes of pontiffs. Here there were only some ivory plaques. Beckford picked one up. His eyes opened wide.

'Byzantine,' he said. 'A carving of the ninth century, I should say. What an exquisite rarity, Mr. Farquhar! I itch to acquire it.'

'I picked it up for a couple of pounds at Philip's auction rooms.'

'Of course. To the ignorant oafs who fancy themselves connoisseurs in this benighted island, this lovely thing would be dismissed as the whittling of a child.' He looked up from the carving. 'How I hate the English, Mr. Farquhar! How I hate them.' He restored the plaque to its cupboard and closed the doors.

'You have admirable taste, Mr. Farquhar,' he said.

'You might say the same, Mr. Beckford, of a jackdaw in whose nest you found a brooch by Cellini.'

'You buy on no principle, then?'

'Sometimes I buy because I like things; more often I buy to stop another man having it.'

There was a long silence in the room as Beckford quizzed treasure after treasure. With an illuminated manuscript in his hands he said, 'You were unwise to let me into your secret room. You will not get rid of me till midnight.'

'In that case you will be obliged, Mr. Beckford, to do me the honour of dining with me.'

'Certainly.'

'Permit me, then, to send word to your coachman. The stables are in Mount Street.' He left the room, closing the door carefully behind him.

When Farquhar returned, he found Beckford, his hands behind his back, staring up at a portrait which hung over the chimney piece. Leaving him undisturbed, Farquhar went to a cupboard and took out two glasses and a bottle. Hearing the noise, Beckford turned.

'By Hoppner, I take it,' said Beckford, nodding towards the picture.

'Partly,' said Farquhar, smiling.

'Yes, indeed. What a damned rogue the man has become! He does the head and leaves the rest to his pupils, as he calls them. I made him do all of me down to my stockings. He made me look like a bookseller. All the same, this is one of his better heads. Who is it?'

'My father.'

'A fine gentleman.'

'Alas, no. Never. He was a carpenter. His great ambition was that *I* should become a gentleman.'

Beckford ran a curious eye over the shabby figure in front of him, but said nothing.

'Permit me to offer you some wine,' said Farquhar.

Beckford hesitated. The cellars of Fonthill were the best in England. It was many years since he had drunk another man's wine. It was many years since any man had offered it.

'You need have no fear, Mr. Beckford. The wine was recommended by Perkins, your own supplier.'

'Then it was recommended by me. That dolt Perkins has the palate of a coal heaver. I've made him a fortune, and now I'm happy to say I owe him one. Thank you. I will take a glass with you.'

Farquhar set two fragile glasses on the table, with delicately distorted stems.

'Murano,' said Beckford.

'Indeed, yes. They were made for the Duke of Urbino in sixteen ... sixteen ... I have forgotten the exact date.'

'And you use them?'

'Only since I discovered that at Fonthill you do not dine off gold plate, as the rumour goes.'

'I certainly do not. That's for belching and farting aldermen at the Guildhall.'

'But,' said Farquhar, pouring the wine, 'you do dine from a superb set of Meissen ware.'

'How did you know? It was not on display.'

'I talked to your cook.'

'You questioned the *servants*?' said Beckford, and mentally noted that he had named him well. Mr. Filthyman would do.

'I'm afraid so,' said Farquhar. 'Not the act of a gentleman, I know, but to my father's lasting distress, I have never managed to be one.' He raised his glass. 'To the Master of Fonthill.'

They drank. They sat. The glasses were refilled. The wine coursing through his veins brought back memories of Portugal to Beckford, of Franchi, young, beautiful and loving, and now fat and still loving. Beckford felt his host's eyes fixed on his, gentle monkey's eyes, grown gentler. He felt a great desire to talk to this dilapidated man, and he did not know why.

'It is curious that your father should have wished you to be a gentleman,' said Beckford. 'So did mine.'

'But you were born one,' Farquhar protested. 'Your father was Lord Mayor of London—twice, I believe.' Beckford smiled. 'Ah, yes. I see. Belching and farting aldermen, yes.'

'I was born into a fortune made from Jamaican sugar,' said Beckford. 'We are a family of tradesmen—I loved my father, passionately. But he had been born in Jamaica. He never lost the ugly accent they use there. He never lost their uncouth gestures. Had he picked up this glass he would have broken it at the first sip. And the gentlemen of England, may God damn them, laughed at him. They laughed at him in the House of Commons. They made fun of him at their tables. He loved talking and arguing. They listened and made witty remarks. My father never understood wit. He would join in the laughter against himself, not understanding the joke—a great, big, bellowing laugh it was, that rattled the glasses on the table and made the footmen snicker. It suited his fellow tradesmen, so they made him mayor. He once met the king on their behalf. He was so uncouth that the king sent him a message afterwards telling him that he hoped no further meeting would ever take place.'

'George the Third preferred talking to trees in Windsor Park,' said Farquhar. 'Trees are very polite.'

'My father thought that if he had a country seat, he would be accepted. He built it. It was a monument to vulgarity. It had a hall like that of an Egyptian temple. There is one in the Mansion House, and for a shilling the beadle will show it to you in all its horror. The house was called inevitably Splendens. It was built at Fonthill. When he died and I inherited, I pulled it down and used its stones to build the Abbey. I built it to show my dead father that I was all he so longed to be—an English gentleman. And the English gentlemen hounded me out of the country.' Beckford looked into his glass. 'Like my father, I do not know when to stop talking.'

Beckford had learned that he should never talk about his troubles. There would be sympathy at first—and Mr. Filthyman was very sympathetic, in spite of his shabbiness, or perhaps because of it. But then would come the slow smile, or the look of amused contempt, or, sometimes, poorly hidden disgust. And then Beckford could feel that it was he himself who was a Mr. Filthyman.

Farquhar was saying, 'So we have two ambitious fathers in common. But there is a great difference between inheriting your wealth, as you have done, and making it oneself, as I did.'

Beckford reflected that the one sure way of keeping silent about one's self and one's ... tastes (and how tempting it was to talk about them), the one sure way was to make the dangerous listener talk about *himself*.

He said, 'How did you make your money?'

Farquhar said, 'Your father was, I believe, a freethinker, a *philosophe*, in the fashion of the times.'

Beckford nodded.

'Mine,' Farquhar went on, 'was a Calvinist. The followers of Calvin, as I need not tell you, believe that some of us are predestined to damnation, while others are chosen by God to be saved. My father believed he was damned. He was very firm about it. He would get angry if he was contradicted. He was certain he would go to hell, and my father's hell was a very real one.'

'I am a firm believer in hell,' said Beckford.

'Indeed you are, sir. Not the least marvel of this exceptional day is that I am in the presence of the author of *Vathek*.'

Beckford's eyes glowed with pleasure. He watched Farquhar go to the bookcase which had fretted decoration in the Gothic taste and take from it a book bound in gold-tooled morocco. Farquhar returned and handed the book to him.

'Ah!' said Beckford. 'You have the French edition. I wrote *Vathek* in French, you know, but a scoundrel pirated an English translation and had the damned impertinence to say it was an unpublished tale from *The Arabian Nights*. I see you have a signed edition. I will sign it again before I go.'

Farquhar bowed his head in acknowledgement.

'Your description of hell in that book,' he said, 'has never been equalled. *Vathek* will live for ever. When people read Dante only to pass examinations, they will read *Vathek* to find out what hell is really like.'

'You see,' said Beckford, in the falsely apologetic tone of an author who has been flattered and wants more of it, 'I have been there, and Dante never convinces me that he has. I am glad you think *Vathek* will live. I am quite sure nothing else I have done will last. But you were telling me about your father.'

Farquhar, wise enough not to change the subject when an author was talking about his writings, protested that the story of his life, now that he came to think of it, would bore his guest. Beckford half closed his eyes.

(*'Commander of the Faithful,'* said the merchant from Aleppo, *'the story of my life and the strange reasons which caused me to amass this treasure only to hide it away, will,*

*I am sure, be tedious to the Master of the World. But, should
you command that I tell it, I shall obey.'*

*('We do command,' said the Caliph Vathek Bi'llah and,
clapping his hands, ordered that more wine be brought for the
merchant and that it should be the finest in the palace.)*

'Tell me about your life,' said Beckford. 'All that I know is
that you have been to India. Tell me about that. Tell me how
you got there and what it was like. I have always dreamed of
going there, but I never went.'

'What prevented you, Mr. Beckford?'

'Something which happened in my boyhood, which I would
rather not recall. Tell me, instead, about yours, and meantime
let us have another bottle of this excellent wine.'

The wine found, Farquhar said, laughing, 'I was a bright
boy with an ambitious father, and that means in Aberdeen
that my boyhood was a painful one. My father sent me to a
school, but I quickly learned all the dominie had to teach me,
which was very little. I worked a while in my father's carpenter's shop, until the pastor of our church took an interest
in me. He offered to continue my education in the evenings,
which I fancy were rather lacking in entertainment for him. It
was his firm belief that boyhood was intended by the Almighty
to be a time of tribulation—indeed, he could preach for
two hours on the subject. A boy must learn that life is a vale
of tears. My personal tears were produced by a thick and long
leather strap, peculiar, I believe, to Scotland, and called the
tawse. It was much in use then, and I believe that the habit
of flogging boys was the only thing about the Scots that the
great Samuel Johnson approved of. True to his principles,
our pastor was not happy unless I lowered my breeches at
his orders at least two or three times in an evening. Perhaps
the Great Lexicographer was right. I wept bitterly at the time,
but I bore no resentment. One of the lessons he beat into me

was that since I was a poor boy with brains, I should use them to make money, and I would never do that in Aberdeen. There were too many Scots doing the same thing. He made me learn a great deal of geography, using my posterior to illustrate my mistakes instead of a terrestrial globe, which he did not have.

'His intention was at first that I should go to England, but at that time—I was now sixteen—all talk was of the great fortunes that men were amassing in the East Indies, many of them Scots, and many starting out as poor as I was, one of them, or so I was told, being General Clive. He carried me to London at his own expense. We spent several days waiting in the outer precincts of the East India Company with no result. But at last, in a casual encounter, we met one of the directors, who, in his youth, had sat under our pastor and listened to his sermons. The meeting was emotional—brimming eyes was a fashion of the time—and I was sent to some functionary to be examined. He tested my knowledge of Latin, Greek, grammar and ciphering. I did not feel I had done well, and I walked the streets of London for a long time, not daring to return to our lodgings. When I did, I found the pastor sitting beside the table, with an inscrutable expression. On the table was the tawse. Old as I was, I began to unbuckle my belt. But the pastor said, "John, my boy, you sail to Bombay by the next ship". I was so overjoyed I embraced him. He got out of my arms and took up the tawse. "Pack this in your luggage," he said, "and when you come back to Aberdeen, bring it with you in a golden box".'

'A charming conceit,' said Beckford. ('*Worthy of the Caliph,*' he said to himself. '*Vathek often whipped his favourite pages.*')

'So you went to Bombay,' said Beckford, thoughtfully. 'It's an island, is it not, that faces the Arabian Sea. I have always imagined that sea to be particularly beautiful; it has such a beautiful name.'

'It is much like any other sea—no, do not look downcast; I shall not disappoint you—any other sea, that is, in the mornings and the evenings and the night. But at about three o'clock in the afternoon, when most people on the island are asleep, it takes on a strange glitter, as though slivers of pure gold and silver had been showered upon it. The Arabian Sea *clothes* itself as though in some rich mantle. Kings, popes and queens have set hundreds of tailors and seamstresses to work for weeks on end so that they should shine with that sudden golden glory, but this sea would make them drab if they should walk on its beaches. It does not last long. It is something to do with the angle of the sun, but I have never seen it elsewhere, and travellers have told me that neither have they.'

'I envy you the sight,' said Beckford.

'For my first few weeks it was my only consolation, because I was very unhappy. It was brought home to me how right my father had been to urge me to make myself a gentleman. The junior clerks lived in a great, rambling bungalow in the fort—that part of the island which the Portuguese had walled off and now belonged to the company. I had won my clerkship on merit. There were five others, and all had got theirs through influence. They, indeed, were gentlemen, sprawling elegantly on the verandas in nankeen breeches which were always spotlessly white, commanding an array of Indian servants with ease. I had never had a servant in my life, and the Indians knew it. I treated the servants as friends, and they despised me; I lost my temper with them, and my fellow clerks despised me in turn. "You don't *quarrel* with servants, John," they would tell me. Meals were an agony. I would either sit quite silently, desperate to think of something to say, or I would talk too much and the other clerks would yawn in my face. Then there were the Hindus. Hindus are divided into a hundred social layers. At the top are the Brahmins, and from then on downward there are castes and castes within castes. The other clerks took all this with ease; they knew to a nicety who was above or below whom and treated them accordingly, and it was a serious matter. One caste will not eat with another, and you can offer a man a deadly insult by asking him to drink a sherbet with somebody beneath him. I blundered all the time; my companions never.'

'They had been brought up among women who spend whole days discussing with whom they will or will not take a dish of tea,' said Beckford.

'I knew nothing of that,' said Farquhar, 'and still know nothing. I have never moved in society.'

'Read Maria Edgeworth,' said Beckford. 'She is most amusing. But I am interrupting you. Please go on.'

'Then there was money,' said Farquhar. 'I had thought my salary was princely, but there were horses to be kept, an army of grooms, carriages and coachmen and runners. There was a largesse to be distributed on innumerable feast days. The other clerks had money of their own, sent out in drafts upon Indian merchants by each ship from England. They would urge me to be generous, to spend, to dress extravagantly, to drink deep and expensively. "We must not let the Hindus outshine us," they would say earnestly, "or they will cut our throats."

'I used to go on long rides on my hired horse to think things out. The Indians are a wonderful people to live among if you want to think. They are handsome to look at, very polite, full of smiles, and yet you feel they do not, deep down, give a tuppenny damn for you. They are too busy with their own affairs. For the first time in my life I did not have to worry about what people thought of me. My fellow clerks were too busy hunting or riding about or getting drunk each night to fight off the heat. The Indians barely knew my name. They called me Chota Sahib, which means "Little Sahib", because I was a junior. When I insisted that they learned my name, they tried, as polite as ever.'

Farquhar smiled. 'It came out as "Fucker",' he said. 'I did not correct them. It amused me to think of the horror of my father and the pastor could they have heard it. Permit me to open another bottle of wine. Ah, I see that the evening is upon us. Allow me to close the curtains. Or perhaps, Mr. Beckford, you would prefer the twilight. It goes with the Gothic taste.'

'It does,' said Beckford, 'and I have had my bellyful of it. There are rooms in Fonthill where you can't see your hand in front of your face at four in the afternoon. Draw the curtains, Fucker Sahib, and shut out England. Take me back to India. The inhabitants sound to my taste.'

'I believe that the Hindus,' said Farquhar, seating himself again and putting two feet in muddy shoes on the ornate table, 'have the secret of a happy life. They are devoutly religious, and their religion has no morals.'

'The best of both worlds,' said Beckford.

'They believe, Mr. Beckford, that the worst punishment the gods can inflict on a man who neglects their worship is to have him born again after he is dead.'

'How exquisitely cynical!' exclaimed Beckford. 'I think they are gods that even the late lamented M. de Voltaire would have worshipped.' He drank off his glass and held it to be refilled. 'And what was the result of your rides among these original people?'

'I saw that my father was mistaken and that my pastor was right. It was no use trying to be a gentleman unless I made

31

money. How was I to make money? Bonaparte called us a nation of shopkeepers. Well, then, I must open a shop.'

'A shopkeeper can never be a gentleman,' said Beckford in a shocked voice.

'Not while he is still behind the counter. So I looked around for something that men always needed, in great quantities, and were prepared to pay for. Resting my horse in the shade of a tree, like Buddha, I found what I was looking for.' He fell silent and drank deeply.

'What was it?' said Beckford.

'What was it that even Bonaparte needed when he was Emperor of the French and master of Europe?'

'Women?' said Beckford vaguely. 'No. You tantalize me. I confess I do not know.'

'Gunpowder,' said Farquhar.

Beckford struck his forehead. 'Of course. How stupid of me not to guess! And how clever of you.'

'Thank you, Mr. Beckford. I really owe it to a hunter who was some little distance away at the time. He was an Englishman, and he fired at a bird, missed and swore. I reasoned that the one thing that people will lavish money on without a stint is war. Wars there will always be, and wars need gunpowder. I made inquiries and found out why the hunter swore. The East India Company's gunpowder was made in India, outside Calcutta. It was poor stuff. My pastor had tawsed a little elementary chemistry into my posterior, for he dabbled himself in it—the thing was in the air; men like Priestley and Cavendish were dabbling, too. I set up a little laboratory in a hut in the compound of our bungalow and experimented. I soon found out what was wrong. I made my own powder. I took it to Calcutta—a stupendous journey, Mr. Beckford, which I made in a leisurely way during my leave, seeing the sights.

The Taj Mahal stands second, in my opinion, only to your own Fonthill.'

'Yes. Yes,' said Beckford testily. 'Do not remind me of the place. What about your gunpowder?'

'The company men in Calcutta were delighted with it. It had more force than theirs and, better still, made more noise. Noise, in Indian wars, was more important than men. Tactics did not depend on the solid square or the flanking attack. They consisted of making your enemies' soldiers run away. Bribery was the usual means, but noise was just as effective, and cheaper. They set me up in a factory, and in the course of the years I prospered. By certain means I sold both to the company and the maharajahs and nabobs. I was, after all, a Calvinist. I did not know which side was saved and which damned. I left that to the Almighty.'

'So you became rich,' said Beckford.

'I returned to England worth half a million pounds. I am worth much more now.'

'It must have been a triumphant return,' said Beckford.

Farquhar looked at his guest for a while, quite silent. At length he said, 'I believe you must know already what happened.'

'Gossip, yes. But gossip—well. Did you *really....*'

'Did I really walk all the way from Gravesend Port to London? Yes, I did. When I arrived in London, I was so begrimed and muddy my bankers refused to honour my draft. Fortunately, I was provided with documents, so I got my money. I can still see the clerk's round eyes when he found out how much I was worth,' said Farquhar, grinning.

Beckford got up and began to pace the room, occasionally picking up some dust-covered work of art, blowing it clean and replacing it. Farquhar watched him silently. Putting back a Pompeiian statuette, Beckford said at last:

33

'You have been kind enough to praise my book. I am an author, Mr. Farquhar, and you have raised my literary curiosity. More, you have inflamed it. You went out to India to become a gentleman. With considerable perspicacity, you made half a million pounds, which is more than a great number of gentlemen have ever seen. You could have burst upon London like the other millionaires who come back from the East and established yourself as a gentleman in a fortnight. Your manners are princely—'

'I learned them from princes,' said Farquhar.

'—with a town house, carriages, twenty servants and a burly Scots footman to knock at front doors, you could have been the most talked-about man in town.'

'I was,' said Farquhar.

'Precisely. Your extraordinary walk, your poverty of dress could not fail to set tongues wagging, to say nothing of your money. As an author, not a gossip, may I ask you why you did it?'

Farquhar smiled broadly. 'With the author of *Vathek*, to hear is to obey. I shall tell *you*, though I have never told anybody else. I shall tell *you*, because we have one thing in common.'

'What is that?'

'I shall tell you that, too—if it really will need telling when it comes to it. But permit me to do so over the finest saddle of mutton in London. It is sent to me daily from Wales. And I have some wine that is worthy of it. You will be relieved to hear I do *not* eat at home. I eat at the King's Arms, and we shall be quite private. The room that is reserved for me has Jacobean panelling which I think will take your eye. And I am sure you will find the service excellent—yes,' he said, smiling again, 'really excellent.'

34

It was not the panelling which took Beckford's eye, but the servant. There was only one to do all the duties. He was an Indian boy of about seventeen, with long lashes shading deep brown eyes, in a face with all the exactly symmetrical beauty of his race. He was dressed in a servant's jacket and dark breeches, but Beckford, eating his saddle of mutton with abstraction, undressed him in his mind and arrayed him in wide, thin trousers, a waistcoat sparkling with gem-set buttons and a turban. Beckford retied the turban several times; he did not get it to his satisfaction until the port was served. Each time Beckford looked at Abdul (for that was what Farquhar called him) Abdul smiled, showing a row of white teeth.

Farquhar was a man who did not talk over his meat. But when Abdul had cleared the plates and left the room, Farquhar said, 'And now shall I tell you why I walked from Gravesend to London?' Then, noticing Beckford was still looking at the closed door, he added, 'Oh, Abdul will come into the story, I promise you: many Abduls.'

Hearing that, Beckford gave his host all his attention.

First, Farquhar described the heat of Bombay in the summer: the way the sun strikes, it seems with a physical force; the humid air; the bouts of languor interspersed with moments of violent irritation. He spoke of the illnesses the heat produced, and he told of the way a newcomer was initiated by the other clerks.

'They drive out to the cemetery with you and make you read the tombstones. So-and-so, died at the age of twenty-two; so-and-so, twenty-three; so-and-so, departed this Earth in his nineteenth year; and the headstone of a veteran of twenty-seven. Then we all drive back, change into Indian clothes, smoke a hookah and get roaring drunk.'

Then the new recruit was taught the rules. He was there for one purpose: to make money for the company. He must

35

never discuss politics or religion. As for this latter, a church was being built in the fort, but amid such indifference that the walls remained no higher than six feet for many years.

There was the question of women. In that hot climate even the most chaste young man found himself a stallion at the most unexpected moments. The wives of the natives were beyond the pale and in any case were in purdah and invisible. The new recruit must conform to the custom of the country. From time to time the clerks would hold a music and dancing party. The clerks did not dance. They sat firmly on cushions, dressed in the cool Indian fashion. Girls did the dancing, while musicians beat drums and scraped at odd-looking instruments. Neither the dancing nor the music meant anything to Western ears except boredom, but protocol was rigid. Although the heat and the lascivious movements of the girls produced an almost unbearable tension in the young men's flowing trousers, it was simply not done to rise from the cushions and fall upon the girls. The word 'girl', the new clerks were informed, could often be taken literally. Some were only eleven or twelve. These, too, were available for love. When the recruit expressed horror at this (as he invariably did), he would be told that after a year in the Bombay climate he would find these children a considerable compensation for being six thousand miles away from home.

Included in the party would be a pimp. This man should be treated with respect, as an English beau would treat his tailor. He would take your measure and flatter your tastes. After an hour or two, this man would give a signal for the music to stop. The dancing girls would then join the clerks, handing them drinks or massaging their feet. Why massaging the feet should be considered erotic would remain one of the mysteries of the East to the recruit until he retired from service. He must assume it was meant to keep women in their place. What he should notice was the expert way in which the pimp sat exactly the girl you desired beside you. No matter how wooden an English face you tried to maintain, he would read your mind.

You could now take your girl off to a bedroom. There were rules here, too. You did not lock your door. It would cause mirth among the servants, who would consider you a shy boy, not a man. Moreover, the servants would pass through the room while you were in the act. To object would again be a sign of effeminacy. When you indicated that you had had enough of lovemaking, the girl would vanish.

'I remember one clerk called Rawlings,' said Farquhar, 'who had made the Grand Tour of Europe when he was nineteen, and he said that this trick of disappearing when it was over was the thing he most admired about Indian whores. He had had sex with their counterparts in Paris, Geneva, Rome, Venice and Naples, and all stayed too long when it was over. Once you had seen the Indian girls in the extraordinary but delectable positions they assumed, it would be ludicrous or embarrassing to see them quietly patting their buns into shape at a mirror. So they went, as if by magic. Payment was made in the morning after breakfast to the pimp, and you paid it with as little shame as you would pay any merchant's bill.'

He called the boy Abdul, who opened another bottle of port. 'Yes,' said Beckford, absently, as he watched the boy, 'it sounds all most convenient, but I am not sure that a life with prostitutes would please me.'

He studied Abdul's slim hips as he bent to retrieve a hand-kerchief from the floor. A warm glow spread through Beckford's body. Rashly he said, 'Besides, I have no great liking for acrobatics though I am very partial to acrobats.'

Instantly he closed his mouth. His loose tongue had got him

37

into trouble so many times. He looked cautiously at Farquhar. There was an expression of extreme geniality on his host's lined face.

'Ah, yes,' said Farquhar. 'Boys. That aptly introduces the second part of my story, if you have the patience to listen to it.'

(*The merchant from Aleppo paused. The Caliph Vathek drew a priceless gem from his finger. 'Accept this as a token of the entertainment we have had from the first part of your tale,' he said. 'Divert us with the second part, which promises to be charming!' The merchant, bowing, said, 'God is great, and Aleppo is a wicked city. My fate was written, and I submitted to His decree.' 'As must we all,' said the caliph testily. 'But I am impatient to hear more about your adventures—proceed.'*)

'Well,' said Farquhar when Abdul had withdrawn, 'after one taste of the entertainment the dancers had to offer, I did not go again. When the others held a gathering, I would walk by the Arabian Sea for a long time and I would not return to the bungalow until the music had finished. One morning I met the pimp on the veranda where he had been collecting his bills. He flung himself on his knees, touched my boots and begged forgiveness. I silently said a prayer of thanks to the Almighty and gently raised him to his feet. There were tears in his eyes. He beat his breast and said he was an old man and a fool. He should have seen that I wanted boys, and if I could forget his stupidity like the magnanimous prince that I was, he had the pick of the boys in Bombay.

'I struck him,' said Farquhar. 'That cost me a guinea in the fines box. Striking the natives was considered bad for business.'

Some weeks after that came the incident of the cummerbund. This was a broad band of black silk that was wound around the waist. The company had adopted it almost as a

38

badge of their calling. On all formal occasions the company men wore full English dress. This presented difficulties. In visiting Hindu or Mogul dignitaries, Englishmen had to sit on cushions and mattresses. The temperature of the room was often very high, and the peacock fan that servants waved cooled the face but not the body. It was necessary after a while to unbutton one's coat. This left an unsightly view of the top of one's breeches. The cummerbund covered this.

It was put on with the aid of an expert servant. This servant stood against the wall of the bedroom, holding one end of the cummerbund, while the Englishman stood several feet away from him, holding the other against his waist. The master then pirouetted towards his servant, winding the cummerbund about him, the servant deftly manoeuvring the silk so that the folds lay perfectly around the stomach and loins. The company men were foppish, having to contend with the gold-embroidered tunics of their Indian hosts, the turbans with their jewelled pins, and the pearls, diamonds, rubies and emeralds with which Indians adorned their person. Much importance was therefore attached to putting on the cummerbund.

The servant boy who did this for Farquhar was a handsome Hindu of seventeen called Munoo. One evening when Farquhar was dressing to go out to play chess with a man of princely rank, Munoo was nowhere to be found. Farquhar shouted his name and clapped his hands, to no effect. Exasperated, he strode out in a temper onto the veranda.

Rawlings was sprawled in a chair, already a little fuddled with his evening whisky. Farquhar asked if he had seen Munoo. Rawlings looked up and smiled slowly. He nodded.

'Then where is he?' demanded Farquhar, and when Rawlings did not answer immediately, he added, 'Please, I am in a great hurry.'

'In there,' said Rawlings, pointing to a door.

Farquhar immediately went to it. The door was unlocked as was the custom. Farquhar pushed it open and strode into the room. Munoo was lying on his stomach on the bed, naked, with one of the company's clerks, also naked, on top of him vigorously seeking his pleasure.

Farquhar, in utter confusion, turned and left the room, closing the door behind him. He stared at Rawlings, unable to speak.

'Have some whisky,' said Rawlings. 'You look as though you need it. And sit down. In the tropics always sit down when in the grip of strong emotion. It lessens the strain on the heart.'

Farquhar, whose knees were weak from the shock, obeyed. There was a long silence between the two men. Farquhar's knees stopped trembling.

'One of the abominations of the Canaanites,' said Rawlings in the tones of a preacher.

A sound came from behind the closed doors.

'Though I never,' said Rawlings in his natural voice, 'I *never* imagined the Canaanites *giggling* while they were being abominable. But you are in a hurry for your cummerbund,' he said. 'I will get my servant to help you.' He clapped his hands, and his elderly servant appeared.

Farquhar lost three games of chess in a row, and his Indian host politely blamed it on the climate. He returned to the bungalow to find Munoo sleeping as usual, outside his bedroom door. He woke him roughly and told him he was dismissed. The boy took the matter calmly and said he would send his brother in the morning so that Farquhar would not miss his 'little breakfast', a ritual meal of a cup of tea and a banana.

Farquhar slept fitfully. He was awakened at six o'clock by

a boy of some fourteen years of quite remarkable beauty.

'Now,' said Farquhar, 'began a series of quite dreadful nights for me. I would go to sleep readily enough, but then I would dream. I would have nightmares in which I would run from some peril I never saw. At other times my father would rate me for some crime for which I did not know. I would be a boy again awaiting punishment from the pastor. Once he tawsed me in my dreams for not being able to spell Canaanite. And again and again I saw those white and brown bodies on the bed. The boy was always laughing, mostly at me. I would wake up with a burning forehead and an aching body. I thought I had caught some fever, but the doctor assured me if I had, it was none that he knew of.

'It was my new servant, Rajan, who found a cure. He would bathe my forehead with cloths dipped in ice-cold water. There was, I need not say, no ice in the bungalows. This was a luxury known only to the Moguls themselves, who had it brought from the Himalayas. But the water in the well in our compound was very cold, provided it was freshly drawn, and this Rajan did for me. I would wake him; he would run and draw water. With great gentleness he would bathe my forehead, and the heat and aches would rapidly pass.

'He was very solicitous. He moved his bed—it was only a doubled-over blanket—next to mine, so I could wake him instantly. He would hold my hand till I went to sleep again. Then one night, after a particularly bad dream, he climbed into bed beside me, embraced me and reached his hand to my groin. I had forgotten to say,' said Farquhar, 'that one symptom of my illness or whatever it may have been was that I always awoke with a massive erection. Rajan said, "Me very good doctor-wallah. You lie still".'

'And he *was*, I may suppose,' said Beckford. 'A very good doctor-wallah.'

Farquhar pursed his lips, then smiled broadly. 'After a few days of his medicine,' he said, 'I was completely cured. But by that time I had quite fallen in love with him. I suppose it was his admirable bedside manner. Women fall in love with their doctors, I'm told.'

'But doctors,' said Beckford with a mischievous grin, 'stay beside the bed. Did Rajan?'

'No,' said Farquhar after some hesitation. 'No. I will be frank: he didn't.'

'Tell me, how do boys manage in a hot climate? Here in England they say, "Oo, it's perishing cold in my bed. Can I come into yours?"'

'They see evil spirits outside the window.'

'I suppose, with your Calvinist's upbringing, you felt guilty?'

'At first, very,' said Farquhar. 'I had learned a little Urdu and Rajan quite a lot of English. But his English didn't go as far as the word "sin". I did manage to explain it to him. He looked very relieved. "Everything all right," he said. "You give me sovereign and everything all right." This seemed to me to be corrupting the boy further. But he clambered off the bed, felt in the pocket of my breeches and took out a guinea. He ran off with it. About fifteen minutes later he came back, grinning broadly, and climbed into bed. "No sin," he said, "all finished. I give gold coin to priest. He say many, many 'Hare Rama' and buy curry and pistachio rice. Rama very fond pistachio rice. No sin," he said and began to make love. Certainly there was nothing on *his* conscience.'

'The Hindus seem to have an admirable faith,' said Beckford.

'Oh, I agree. I took up the study of it with some enthusiasm. A learned Brahmin instructed me. When I told him about my conscience, he advised me to go with Rajan to a much venerated holy man. He had an immense white beard, and he was quite naked. My instructor went with me. He explained the situation. The holy man suddenly roared what might have been either a prayer or an imprecation, took off his slipper and chased Rajan three times around the temple, striking him whenever he could. Rajan disappeared. The holy man returned, panting. When he had recovered his breath, he intoned something in what I recognized as Sanskrit. I asked my Brahmin what it was. He replied, "The swami said, 'It is always the boy who seduces the man.' It is a very old proverb." '

Beckford laughed loudly. 'And a very wise one,' he said. 'How long did your love affair with Rajan last?'

'Not very long. His wife had a difficult pregnancy, and he was very worried. You see, he had been married when he was twelve. When I heard this, it quite took—well, the gilt off the gingerbread. I had come to think that loving a boy was, in a way, romantic, but when he turned out to be a married man, it was a very difficult matter.'

'Yes,' said Beckford. 'To commit sodomy and adultery at the same time would have been embarrassing. You gave him up then?'

'Yes.'

'Were there others?'

'Many. Asoka, my laboratory assistant, who had such delicate hands; Lakshman, who wore his wide trousers so well; Ibrahim, who had such beautiful teeth; Krishna, of the slim, slim hips,' he went on lyrically. 'Shekar—ah, Shekar.' He broke off, staring at the wall.

'What was his special gift?' asked Beckford.

'Eh?' said Farquhar, pulling himself together. 'Who? Oh, Shekar. I don't think he had any. He was an elephant boy. He looked so small sitting on his enormous animal that it

43

made me quite sentimental.' Farquhar's face grew serious.
'Shekar was the last,' he said.

Beckford stayed silent, listening intently.

'I had moved to Calcutta by then,' continued Farquhar. 'I
had made a pile of money. Then a ship's captain called
Macpherson made friends with me. I suppose because he was
Scots or because I was growing homesick, we became very
close, seeing each other every day. I opened out my heart to
him. I confessed about the boys. He was very broad-minded
about it all and pressed me for details. He wrote them all
down, posted the letter to a clergyman in Aberdeen, who told
my father. My father had a sudden heart attack. He fell
face forward on the table, his mouth open, and quite dead. So
they tell me.

'I was quite sure I had killed my father as surely as if I
had killed him with a shotgun. I was prostrated with grief
and guilt. My English doctor tried to rally me. He said he
had performed hundreds of autopsies, and never had he found
the cause of death to be an errant son or an unfaithful wife.
I saw what he meant, but it did not relieve me. My Indian
friends were more helpful. The Hindus among them said it
was due to something my father had done in a previous life
and it was pointless and vain to think one could alter a man's
Karma by one jot. My Moslem friends said it had all been
written on the leaves of a tree by Allah, long before either of
us were born. Perhaps if I had stayed in India, I might
have come close to thinking like the Indians. But I caught
a fever which I could not throw off. My doctor warned
me that if I did not want to join the others in the cemetery, I
should go back to England. I was thirty—old for an Englishman in the tropics. I had a fortune, made from my gunpowder.
I took ship and sailed for England.'

The voyage had taken three months. Farquhar's doctor

44

had assured him that the sea air would do him good. Unfortunately the captain was a gloomy man, much affected by indigestion. After the very first dinner aboard he told Farquhar that the ship was a floating Sodom and that all the ships on the India run were the same. Farquhar retreated to his cabin and spoke to no one save his steward for the entire voyage. The nearer England came, the greater waxed his sense of guilt. It was as though he were tearing leaves off a calendar, the final day of which was the Day of the Last Judgment. A hundred schemes of reparation passed through his mind. He considered giving away all his money. But as England approached, league by league, so did Scotland, and his Aberdeen upbringing asserted itself. If the sin of sodomy had killed his father, Farquhar was sure that his son's giving away half a million pounds to boot would cause him to rise from the grave. Besides, his father's dearest wish was that his son would become a gentleman, and money was needed for that.

As the ship beat its way up the English Channel and the Day of Judgment loomed very near, Farquhar remembered that his Hindu friends had told him that some men made up their minds to escape the cycle of rebirth and to wash away the faults of all their reincarnations. They took a vow of poverty. They dressed in the poorest of clothes; they let their hair grow untended till it was matted; and then, looking like the most indigent of their fellows, they walked the length and breadth of the country, ending in the Himalayas. There they found spiritual solace amid the eternal snows. The idea seemed most attractive, but as he sailed past the cliffs of Dover, he saw that there were difficulties. In India men craved blessings of these holy tramps. In England Farquhar would probably be whipped and sent on to the next parish, and compared to the Himalayas, Ben Nevis had a marked lack of spirituality. But the idea stayed with him until the ship tied up at Gravesend.

'It was extraordinary, Mr. Beckford,' said Farquhar, 'most extraordinary. The moment my feet were on the quay, I knew what I would do—to please my father, to please my pastor and to punish myself. I wouldn't give my money away: I would make even more so that one day I could set up as the finest gentleman in the land. But I would have none of its pleasures for myself until I had doubled my fortune. I would dress poorly. I would be as unkempt as the poor. I would have no retinue of servants or carriages. I would have no luxuries whatever. Lighter in spirit than I had been for many months, I set out to *walk* to London, like those Hindus who had pointed the way for me. And that is the origin of all the stories about me.'

Beckford looked into his glass.

'But few poor people drink this vintage port and have superb saddles of mutton brought in from Wales.'

'Mr. Beckford,' said Farquhar with great simplicity, 'I doubled my fortune seven years ago. You recall that my money was principally in gunpowder. I have been fortunate to live in an age of heroes. God bless the Duke of Wellington,' he said, raising his glass. 'The amount of gunpowder that man used up staggered even me.'

Beckford could suppress his excitement no longer. He got up and began to pace about the room. Farquhar rose too.

'My dear sir,' said Farquhar, 'I have kept you too long with my gossip. I can see you are anxious to leave.'

'No, no,' said Beckford. He pressed his hands on Farquhar's shoulders. 'Sit down, Mr. Farquhar, I pray you. Let us refill our glasses. I have questions to ask you.'

Both men sat. The bottle was passed.

'So your penance is over?' said Beckford.

'Quite over.'

'You have no feeling of guilt about Shekar, Rajan—all that.'

'None whatever. I found Abdul here at the docks. A beautiful boy, don't you think?'

'Most handsome. But what about the other part of your resolve? To become a gentleman.'

'I tried, Mr. Beckford,' said Farquhar sadly, 'but I was over sixty when my penance was finished, and a man of that age does not easily change his habits. I looked around for a country house but could not decide. You have been so kind as to say I have taste. I went to the auction sales and bought. As you have seen for yourself, I do not know what to do with them. They say it takes two generations to make a gentleman —and—'

Beckford hit the table. His eyes shone.

'I can make one in two minutes,' he said. He put his hand in his pocket. He took out a ring from which dangled keys.

'These are the keys of Fonthill, Mr. Farquhar. Buy it, and at a stroke you will be the finest gentleman in the land. Everything is there, all in its proper place. Buy it, for the sake of your father, Mr. Farquhar. I will sell it to you for three hundred thousand pounds cash—and you may keep all the servants.'

Farquhar stared at him. 'But the sale . . . Mr. Christie. . . .'

'I shall cancel it. And as for Mr. Christie, I shall, with great pleasure, personally throw him out of the house.'

'Three hundred thousand pounds,' said Farquhar.

'Yes.'

'Cash?' asked Farquhar.

'Yes.'

'And I,' said Farquhar almost to himself, 'will be the finest gentleman in the land.'

47

'And I,' said Beckford entirely to himself, 'will be able to spit in the eye of all those people who think I am a madman who has bankrupted himself building a folly. I shall get back every penny I spent on it and make a profit of seventy thousand pounds. How furious everybody will be.'

Aloud he said, 'Why not come to Fonthill and see it? You do not know the splendour of the Eastern Wing. I have not opened it to the public, because that is where I live. Join me, Mr. Farquhar. I can carry you there tomorrow.'

Farquhar, bemused, said, 'It will be an honour.'

PART TWO

The Scandal

FARQUHAR agreed to go to Fonthill the next day, but as he walked—as was his habit—on foot to Beckford's town house, his old woman carrying a single small bag of luggage behind him, he had misgivings. On his first visit to Fonthill he had gone by mail coach, and as usual he had thought what a deplorable means of conveyance it was. A jolting box, airless or freezing, a mixed company of which one always had a passion for the sound of his own voice; stops, calculated with savagery so that one's bladder was bursting for miles, or one had no need of the stop; execrable meals; and the humour (the worst trial of all) of the coachmen.

Approaching Beckford's house at the appointed hour, he saw six coaches surrounded by a crowd of servants, either liveried or dressed in the finest clothes. There was bustle and shouting, while Beckford, imperious, stood at the top of the steps that led to the front door, giving orders about loading. The coaches were elegantly painted and all emblazoned. The horses were fine. But it was still, Farquhar reflected, two days at least in a coach, with all its attendant miseries.

Beckford greeted him with warmth but broke off to swear roundly at a servant who was clumsy with a case.

'Bohemian glass and look at the way that gorilla is handling it,' said Beckford, and agilely ran down the steps to aid the man.

At that moment, with a shout and a cracking of whips, a

coach drove into the square such as Farquhar had never seen before. It had four wheels and four horses, but the body held two persons and no more. It was high on its springs, like the curricles which young bloods used for dashing about town and the park, but it was much more solid-looking, and it had a high, curving hood. Two footmen sat behind. The whole had verve and elegance, enhanced by the bright paintwork and the polished brass of its fitments.

'You like my britska,' said Beckford at his side.

'Usually I dislike coaches,' said Farquhar, 'but this ... what did you call it?'

'A britska. The English cannot cook, and they cannot make coaches. They are as heavy as their puddings. This is German, the latest. Like Fonthill, it will make my enemies green with envy. I am sorry you will not have it when you buy Fonthill. I have given it to Franchi for being a good boy. Ah, here he is, all ready to start. May I present the Chevalier Gregorio Fellipe Franchi? Gregorio, Mr. John Farquhar, who I hope will be the new owner of Fonthill.'

The 'good boy' was in his fifties. He had a round face and a double chin, but his eyes were young, and so was his dress, the latter deliberately so. He wore the plain coat and narrow trousers that had come into fashion with the Romantics. He wore no stock, but an open shirt with a wide collar. His hair was windswept, or what little of it the wind could sweep.

'I *heard* about you this morning at breakfast,' he said to Farquhar in a high voice, his syllables following quick upon one another's heels. Then, turning upon Beckford, he said, 'How could you think of such a thing, Barzaba, my dear? So typical of Barzaba. You'll break poor, dear Mr. Christie's heart. What a *fool* he will look if Mr. Farquhar buys Fonthill from under his nose.'

'From under hundreds of other noses,' said Beckford with a satisfied smile.

The chevalier gave a short, high-pitched laugh. 'Yes,' he said. 'I thought *that* would amuse you. Naughty Barzaba, *as usual.*'

'Well,' said Beckford, patting the chevalier affectionately on his shoulder. 'We must be off. Take Mr. Farquhar with you in your britska. I shall travel in my coach.' He made off towards a coach with all the blinds drawn down and disappeared into it. At this sign, all his attendants—and Farquhar could count at least a dozen at a glance—climbed aboard. Farquhar and the chevalier followed into the German novelty.

'I think it is going to rain,' said Franchi. 'And even if it isn't, I cannot resist showing you *this*,' he said. He pulled a lever, and from the top of the hood a glass screen, divided into many panels, descended in front of them.

'Now pull up that leather apron and we shall be ever so comfortable.' That done, he said, 'Isn't this *snug*? Wasn't it so very, very kind of Beckford to buy it for me? Well, *buy* isn't exactly the word, because I don't know when we can pay for it. Oh, but then, of course, you're going to buy Fonthill, aren't you? How splendid to be so rich!'

'I don't know that I really am that rich,' said Farquhar. 'Three hundred thousand pounds is a lot of money.'

'*How* much?' said the chevalier, his voice rising to a falsetto.

Farquhar repeated the sum.

'Naughty Barzaba,' said Franchi under his breath.

'Monsieur le Chevalier,' began Farquhar, but Franchi quickly turned the subject of the conversation.

'I'm not French,' said Franchi. 'I'm Portuguese. I'm not really a chevalier either. Barzaba—that's Beckford, I call him that—Barzaba and I have been *together* for years, ever since I was a choirboy and Barzaba—er—I mean. . . .'

'Fell in love with you,' said Farquhar.

'Oh, thank goodness,' said Franchi. 'Barzaba said you were one of *us*, but you never know. You must be careful. That's what I'm always telling Barzaba. "Be *careful*," I say. You think he would have learned his lesson, but he hasn't. No, I'm not really a chevalier. But Barzaba lost his temper one day when I was about twenty-five and said, "It's true the king gave you a title." Well, he's spent hundreds of thousands of pounds in my country, you know. They like him. Portuguese like anybody with money. So they made me a chevalier. I don't think it means much. It's what they call Knights Templar. Of course, when I read about the things *they* got up to, I sometimes think His Majesty was having his little joke. . . . But Barzaba was pleased, and that's what matters.'

'You are very fond of him,' said Farquhar.

'Ever since I met him,' said Franchi, with simplicity. 'More than ever now that he's fallen on hard times. He looked at me with such sad eyes. I was just a boy, but I knew he wanted someone to love him. His mother was a dreadful woman. She came from the English aristocracy and could never forget it. Of course she married for his father's money, and she felt everybody said so. She was always driving Barzaba to be a little gentleman. His father was always driving him to have a brilliant career: Prime Minister or Lord Chancellor or something. His father, you see, was Lord Mayor of London.'

'Twice, I believe,' said Farquhar.

'Exactly. You take my point, Mr. Farquhar. I mean, to be lord mayor once is interesting. The robes and the turtle soup. But *twice*: I mean you can have enough of turtle soup, can't you?'

Farquhar smiled. 'You are most engaging, Chevalier. Tell me more of the young Mr. Beckford.'

'Well,' said Franchi, willingly, as the britska rolled on with remarkable smoothness, 'the double lord mayor had ambitions for his son, but that isn't love, is it? His father was always saying, "My son, you are going to have the best that money can buy," and he was as good as his word. That's how Beckford came to have his first love affair. He was five, and his father wanted him to learn the piano. So he got him a teacher. It happened that the best that money could buy at that time was a boy of seven.'

'Seven?' said Farquhar. 'A piano teacher aged seven.'

'Yes. His name was Mozart. Wolfgang Amadeus Mozart. Have you ever heard of him?'

'Not for many years. He was a prodigy, wasn't he?'

'He was. But he's quite forgotten now. I believe he died loaded with debts. Well, up like a rocket and down like the stick, I always say. Such a *pretty* rocket, too, according to Barzaba.'

Little Beckford had waited impatiently in the great white and gold music room, but the boy prodigy had been very late. Beckford had been taught that a gentleman should never allow himself to be kept waiting without administering a rebuke. He rehearsed his greeting several times in his piping voice. 'Mr. Mozart, you are very late.' He also rehearsed the frown that must go with it, in one of the vast baroque mirrors of which the room was full.

But when at long last a footman flung open the door and said, 'Master Mozzer and tutor to see Master Beckford,' young Beckford could not utter a word. He was struck with wonder at the boy before him. It was not only the assured way he came into the room or the superb tilt of his small chin. It was his eyes, darting intelligence, and his lips, now curved in a smile, part greeting and part disdain. It was also the way he was dressed: the high wig, dazzlingly white, and curled with an art that Beckford had never seen in England; his cravat, starched into fantasies of folds; his jacket, fitting his slim hips to show off his boyish contours; the small sword with its golden pummel; the silk breeches, amber-coloured and gleaming, with chased metal buttons at the knees; the stockings, so smooth that Beckford dropped his eyes to his own, for they felt impossibly wrinkled, a gesture which brought his own English shoes into his view. Beside those of the prodigy, they seemed like boats.

Mozart did not apologize, nor did Beckford rebuke him, because he was already in love.

Mozart bowed; Beckford ducked his head, stuck out his bottom and felt like a country clown. The man with the boy was large and also splendidly dressed, but Beckford was scarcely aware of him, for he was eating Mozart with his eyes.

The man cleared his throat noisily, bowed, and said, in English, but with heavy accent, 'Permit me to introduce myself.' He gave a name which instantly went out of the boy's memory. 'I am a concert manager, but I have come to translate for the maestro.'

The vision opened its lips. The idol was addressing his worshipper, but in German.

'Permit me,' said the concertmaster. 'The maestro said, "Do you speak German?"'

Beckford said, 'No,' then realizing he had made no sound, said, 'No,' again, this time in a shaming squeak.

Mozart said something, and the manager translated, as he did throughout the meeting, woodenly.

'Permit me. The maestro said, "Why do you not speak German? Your king does."'

'He doesn't,' said Beckford.

'He does,' said Mozart.

'He doesn't.'

'He does. Do you know him?'

Beckford shook his head.

'I do,' said Mozart. 'He is my friend. I have played for him twice, and he has walked in the garden with me.'

Beckford gazed reverently at this beautiful boy who walked with kings. His heart beat quickly under his jacket—his dreary dun jacket.

'And,' said Mozart, 'he speaks German. Do you know why?'

Beckford shook his head again.

Mozart gave a wicked smile. His eyes flashed. 'Because he *is* German.'

'He isn't.'

'He is.'

'He isn't.'

'He is.'

'He can't be,' said Beckford, finding words. 'He is King of England.'

'The King of England is a German,' said Mozart. He laid a delicate hand on the hilt of his sword. He shook the wrist of his other hand so his lace ruffles danced. 'Fancy not being able to find a king of your own.'

The manager translated this but shook his head sadly at the prodigy. He spoke to him.

'He is a very good king,' said Mozart, making amends, but reluctantly. 'He is very kind.'

'Good,' said the manager, in the boy's language.

'And he is *German*,' said Mozart, in painful but decisive

English. He walked to the centre of the music room with all the assurance of one who had already walked on concert platforms in the principal cities of Europe. Beckford, trotting a little, followed him. Mozart looked around the room.

'Is your father very rich?' he asked in his native tongue.

'He's the richest man in England.'

'I bet,' said Mozart, 'he's not as rich as my friend the king.'

'He is. He's richer.'

'He's not.'

'He is.'

'How much richer?'

'A *million* times richer!'

The older boy laughed. He patted Beckford on his curly head. Beckford's heart leaped with joy and instantly sank back because he was not wearing a wig. Mozart went over to the clavichord, opened it, then sat at it. He ran his fingers over the keys and then played, with masterly dexterity, a very fast rondo. Beckford, round-eyed, thought it was an angel playing on a harp.

Mozart stopped. He spoke crossly in German to the manager, who replied, but to no effect, since Mozart imperiously stamped his elegant small foot and repeated what he had said. The manager sighed windily; he turned to Beckford.

'The maestro says the piano is not satisfactory.'

'It is the best that money can buy,' said Beckford.

'I am sure,' said the manager, 'but the maestro always—'

'No good. No good,' said the maestro in English. 'This'— he banged the lid—'no good. Bad. Bloody bad. Me, Mozart, lesson no give.' He shut the lid.

Beckford gazed at his idol. Mozart stood up. Tears came into Beckford's eyes, more and more of them until they were running down his cheeks.

Mozart watched for a moment. Then, seizing a ruffle, he gently dried the tears from Beckford's cheeks. He put his arm around the boy's waist.

'Clavichord good,' he said. 'Come,' then his voice ringing, 'Wolfgang Amadeus Mozart give lesson.'

Unbelievably, Beckford found himself sitting next to this god, his own woollen breeches up against the maestro's shapely thigh clad in its impeccable silk. He fell more deeply in love than ever.

'Of course,' said Franchi in the britska, 'it didn't last. None of Beckford's love affairs ever have, except the one with me. That's because I understand him. Only two people have ever done that, me and Margaret.'

'Margaret?' Farquhar asked.

'His wife,' said Franchi. 'Lady Margaret Gordon, the Earl of Boyne's daughter. Otherwise known as Margie, at least to Barzaba and me.' Franchi giggled. 'You see the joke, Mr. Farquhar?'

'Ah—er—joke, yes, Margie. Not the sort of nickname you would expect for the daughter of an earl.'

'*That's* not the joke. Don't you know what a Margie is? Oh, how innocent you are, Mr. Farquhar! A Margie is what we call one of those boys who dress up as women and hang about the Strand.'

'I see,' said Farquhar, 'but Lady Margaret was not, I take it, a boy dressed up as a woman. Or was she?'

'What a delicious thought, you wicked man. That's exactly what Barzaba should have done. You see, after Wolfgang went away on one of his tours, Beckford kept falling in love with every pretty boy he saw. They wouldn't send him to school because of it, so he made do with tutors. But then things got too hot, so the family decided to marry him off.

So they threw Margie at him, and Beckford married her. He was only twenty, and boys are putty in the hands of their female relatives at that age, aren't they? They don't even know what is happening to them. I mean, they're middle-aged before they realize what *schemers* women are when it comes to arranging marriages, and then it's only because they see their own wives doing it. So Barzaba married. But what a delightful thing it would have been if he'd married a Margie. What a wonderful joke. A typical Barzabian joke. Married! In Salisbury Cathedral; with a *bishop*. They live together for a year,' said Franchi, clapping his hands. 'But then what?'

'The Margie runs away,' offered Farquhar.

'Splendid! Whom with? No, don't tell me. She runs off with a grenadier.'

'Most convincing. He—she—probably would, too. They run off to Italy and are never heard of again.'

'So Barzaba is a deserted husband,' said Franchi.

'And everybody would say, "Poor Beckford. You can't blame him. He'll never trust another woman in his life." '

They both broke into peals of laughter. Then Franchi said, 'What a lovely ride we're having. And look, it's raining. Aren't we *snug* with this window in front of us? Tuck up the apron, dear. Here, let me do it for you.'

They drove through the rain a while in silence.

'I suppose the marriage to the real woman was a disaster?' said Farquhar.

'On the contrary, it was a huge success.'

'You astonish me.'

'It always astonishes *me*,' said Franchi. 'Beckford was deeply fond of her. She's dead, of course.'

'Did she know about the boys?'

'Oh, yes.'

'Didn't she object?'

'Not in the least.'

'She must have been an extraordinary woman,' said Farquhar.

'I dare say she was,' said Franchi. He yawned elaborately. 'Don't let's go on talking about her, it makes me jealous. Ask Beckford. He'll talk about her by the yard.'

In his coach behind, Beckford, alone, drew a corner of the window curtain, noted their progress and let it fall again. He composed himself for a reverie. The closed coach, the footmen behind, the coachmen in front, the four strong horses—all gave him a sense of being protected from the world that he could find nowhere else, except on the top storey of the tower at Fonthill. He began to order his thoughts, dropping away from the present, searching into the past.

(The Indian magus slipped the ring with its massive turquoise onto the Caliph's finger. 'Commander of the Faithful, you have but to turn the ring to summon whom you will, be they dead or be they alive, before you. But you may turn it only once. Consider, and be wise.' 'Whom would a wise man summon up?' asked the Caliph, for he feared his thoughts were straying into voluptuous paths. 'The companions of his youth,' said the magus, 'as they were.' 'That, indeed, is wisdom,' said the Caliph, and turned the ring.)

'Iskander,' said Beckford aloud, and closed his eyes.

Alexander Cozens had come into his life when Beckford was a stripling of fourteen. He was an artist, but much more than an artist, at least to a boy. He had a dark, handsome face, large expressive eyes and a curving nose. He talked with great animation and charm, especially to young people, an art he had learned when a drawing master at Eton. But that had been a passing phase in a life which, as he unfolded it to Beckford, glowed with romance.

He had been born in Russia. To young William this meant snow, sleighs and desperate escape from wolves. Cozens at first disclaimed any such adventures but in a manner which led Beckford to disbelieve him. With boyish stubbornness, he set out to make this fascinating tutor talk. After a failure or two he found that if he and Cozens were alone—in the woods, for instance—and if Cozens put his arm around his waist, and if he, young William, put his head on Cozens' shoulder, Cozens would tell stories of his Russian boyhood in which there were pack upon pack of ravening wolves.

Cozens had also known the Czar of All the Russias. He seemed unwilling to enlarge upon this friendship, and William realized that such a man would be the repository of secrets of state about which his lips were sealed, especially to a chattering boy. But young William found that when they went to a secluded pool and William, at Cozens' suggestion, bathed in the Russian manner (presumably in the Russian summer manner) and took off all his clothes, afterward, as he lay beside Cozens, it turned out that Cozens had been the agent of many clandestine dealings with England, an emissary of the czar, with immediate access to the English Prime Minister. Unfortunately the French got wind of this and made more than one attempt on his life. The mark of a bullet in the thigh was there to prove it. In fact, it was all just as William had supposed.

Cozens had also spent many years in the East. Beckford's father always referred to him as the Persian and that, too, had been his nickname at Eton. William called him that to himself at first. But when, one day, Cozens told him how he had followed Alexander the Great's route all the way to the Indies, William named him Iskander, for that was what he was called in the East.

Autumn having set in, there was no more swimming in the

nude. But it was pleasant to sit by the great fire in William's bedroom, the candles unlit, arms around each other's waists, while Cozens talked of the palaces of Persia, the shah-in-shah, the jewelled thrones, with mechanical birds of gold that twittered, sang, and flapped their wings. Delightful, too, to hear of the flowing dresses of the men, the profusion of diamonds, the gold plate on which one ate and the semi-transparent trousers of the pageboys of the courts of Persia and India.

William, at first, imagined all these things as he stared into the fire. But soon that was not necessary, for Cozens brought a portfolio to William's bedroom. It contained paintings, small but exquisitely painted on parchment, done, said Cozens, in Fathepur-Sikri for the Moguls. They showed the monarchs at play: hunting, riding and copulating with their concubines. Others showed them entwined with handsome, doe-eyed boys in, as Cozens pointed out, the uniform of the pages of the court, which was, as he had again pointed out, semi-transparent trousers.

Then came the evening when Cozens had brought a great bundle of the sort of clothes which were illustrated in the miniatures. Eagerly William stripped and allowed Cozens to dress him as a page. Eagerly he responded to the kisses and hugs of Cozens, now arrayed in a turban, though otherwise in his European clothing, he seeming to be in haste.

The semi-transparent trousers having revealed that William, in spite of his banal birth in London, was every bit as potent as the Persian boys, William allowed himself to be led to the bed, and there in peril of the executioner's sword, he surrendered himself to his master, the Grand Mogul, who must not be disobeyed.

William Beckford came out of his reverie as he rode in his coach, drew a curtain and noted they had made good progress. He let fall the curtain and smiled to himself. The seduction had been a very simple affair. Like the schoolmaster he had been, Cozens did no more to boys than they do to themselves, and so it had been with young William on the bed. The semi-transparent trousers had been creditably ruined: the Great Mogul had unbuttoned his white buckskin breeches, but remembering the urgent advice of certain fellow masters at Eton about the perils of indecent exposure, he had thought better of it and buttoned them up again. As for William, he lay back in the pillow dreamily, shut his eyes, slipped off to sleep and dreamed he heard a clavichord playing and a boy's voice saying, 'Goot. Vunce more. *Vun* and two and tree and. . . .'

Then came the snow and the city they built in it. The city was Cozens' notion. It covered a wide area of a clearing on a hilltop remote from any house. It had places—blocks of snow set with stones—houses in narrow streets, mosques with domes and minars, a marketplace with stalls that sold the cargo of countless caravans coming from far-off China or India. Above all, it had its great tower, built by the command of the Caliph. It was eight feet high, and Cozens and William had stood on logs to make its top storey.

William named the place Iskanderbad. It was very vivid in their minds. They knew every alley and could wander in it, hand in hand, even when it was a mile away. They invented a history: one of sieges, rebellions, cruel tyrants, earthquakes and pestilences. A badger with a lair nearby lent colour to these changes by blundering through it at night, and thus many buildings fell under the hand of war or by the passage of time. But the tower stood.

Cozens, with the common sense of a much-travelled man, had seized several occasions to impress on William that no one must know of their lovemaking. He opened William's young eyes to the puritanism that surrounded them. They were not in Ispahan, or Delhi, or Baghdad, but in puritan England. They were alone, surrounded by people who could turn upon the instant into enemies and persecutors.

So at William's suggestion, they took refuge in the Great Tower of Iskanderbad. They furnished it, in their imaginations, with Oriental splendour. In its rooms, wines gushed perpetually, bowls heaped with rare viands stood on marble tables. Discreet servants came and went, disappearing behind great tapestries, glowing with colour. They reclined on silken couches and told tales or listened to them. Far, far below them was the human race.

Thus it was, after making love, each would lie still; each would go into the tower. Each would be protected from a world that, if it knew of what they had done, would destroy them.

Beckford came out of his reverie as, with a great jolting and grinding, his coach came to a halt. Beckford drew aside a corner of the curtain and saw that they had pulled up at an inn. His servants poured from their coaches, making a great bustle and clamour to inform everyone within earshot that their master was important.

Beckford leaned back among the cushions, waiting for a fitting reception to be prepared. Poor Cozens was dead, now, dead in exile and disgrace. The world had destroyed him. But Beckford had built their tower in Fonthill, and he had taken refuge there when the world had tried to destroy him too.

The procession of carriages had arrived the next day very late, when it was quite dark. Farquhar, tired by the long journey, had gone straight to bed.

He spent the morning driving around the estate at Fonthill.

He did it in a small and comfortable carriage drawn by a pony. Beckford held the reins, sitting beside him. As he set out, Beckford had said, 'I have gone to a lot of trouble and expense to ensure that there is nothing to see,' and from then on was silent.

For a while Farquhar was puzzled; there seemed indeed little to see. Farquhar had been driven around many a great estate, largely by men who wanted to borrow money off him, but he had never seen one like this. There were no arbours, no mock ruins, no fake temples, no fountains and no avenues of trees drawn up in lines like soldiers. There was only one road worthy of the name, and that led abruptly to the Great West Door of the Abbey, and they quickly left it. Instead they travelled along winding paths, grass-grown and quiet, under large trees that seemed to be planted in no order.

Then Farquhar began to notice every so often, through these casual trees, a glimpse of the Abbey—its tower, its great oriel window, its turrets and pinnacles—and each of these glimpses had all the harmony of a landscape by that artist whose canvases he had bought.

'Mr. Constable should have painted that,' he ventured, when they were passing one bushy view.

'*I* painted it,' said Beckford. 'Constable can only copy nature. I invent it.'

He drove on silently for a while. Then he said:

'I made a study of parks when I began Fonthill. They are usually the acme of vulgarity. The Italians use them to show off the antique statues, which are mostly fakes. The French turn them into promenades to show off their clothes. The English use them to show off their money. So I decided to make a park which would look as though I have never been here, except to build the Abbey. I wanted to surround my Abbey with land such as it must have looked in the

Middle Ages, before too many people and too much money had ruined the countryside. I created this garden like God, who was not interested, I believe, in parterres and terraces. I have created the most beautiful and natural landscape in all England. And these ignorant swine who have been writing about me in the newspapers praise my Abbey to the skies and do not say a word about the park.'

He drew up and pointed to a perspective that gave on to the Great West Door, showing only its upper half.

'How beautiful!' said Farquhar.

'To make that, I had only to cut down four trees. But it took me two months to decide which trees to fell. But come, we must return to the Abbey. We dine at three, and we must change our clothes.'

This put Farquhar in a quandary for the remaining part of the drive. So great was his admiration for his host that he had made up his mind to clean his nails before dinner, but he had no plan for anything further.

They drew up at the great door and went inside. All trace of the visitors had been removed from the carpet, in the middle of which now stood a marble table which Farquhar had not noticed in his previous visit. On it stood two tall ewers of Sarcenic design, a jewelled sword and a leather-bound book.

Beckford went to the table, picked up the book, opened it at its title page and gave it to Farquhar. Farquhar saw that it was a copy of *Vathek* more handsomely bound than his own. On the title page was written: 'To John Farquhar. The thought that the day is not distant when all that I have done or am doing will dissolve into thin air fills me with the bitterest melancholy.—William Beckford.'

Beckford looked at his guest with the saddest of expressions. 'I wrote that while the servants were sweeping this carpet clear of the bestial *spoor* of Christie's private viewers. Only *you*, Mr. Farquhar, can lift that bitter melancholy from the author of *Vathek*.'

'Dear me, yes, I see,' said Farquhar with a worried look.

'You have decided?' said Beckford.

'Decided? No, not decided. Fonthill overwhelms me with its beauty. Your park is a masterpiece. Indeed, sir, I do see that to have your treasures scattered and your park—er—dotted with Greek temples would be a tragedy.' His eyes gleamed briefly with the light of the marketplace. 'Of course, two hundred thousand pounds cash is a lot of money, with business so bad and no wars to speak of going on and....'

'*Three* hundred thousand pounds,' said Beckford firmly.

'Um,' said Farquhar, quite quelled by Beckford's blazing look.

(*The Caliph Vathek's countenance was pleasing and majestic, but when he was angry, one of his eyes shone with such a terrible light that no man could endure its gaze, and the wretch on whom it turned fell back in confusion and sometimes even expired on the spot.*)

Farquhar had taken a step backward, but he was still on his feet. Beckford-Vathek softened his terrible gaze.

'You will need time, Mr. Farquhar, of course. Meantime, accept the book as a token of my regard for the only man I have ever met who is as original as myself.'

Farquhar bowed.

Farquhar said, rising, 'I am most deeply grateful for the book. I shall treasure it.'

'I trust,' said Beckford, smiling, 'you will treasure it on one of those shelves,' and pointed. 'And now let us change our clothes.'

Farquhar adroitly turned the remark. 'As for changing my clothes, Mr. Beckford, I regret that that will merely mean

66

putting on my second-best pair of breeches. I have no other coat but this.'

Beckford laughed, his loud laugh that went so oddly with his habitually sad expression.

'Mr. Farquhar, we are both men who indulge our fancies. Now, shall I indulge your fancy or shall you indulge mine?'

'As a guest in your house, Mr. Beckford, I should be happy to indulge yours, but—'

'Then you shall. I shall send the Turk to your bedroom immediately.'

When Farquhar got to his room he found the Turk waiting for him, as Beckford had promised. Farquhar had dawdled on his way, examining this and that treasure under the gilded vaults of the Abbey, but with his thoughts elsewhere. He wondered what shape Beckford's fancy would take. Stories of the orgies that were supposed to take place in Fonthill came into his mind. He was alarmed. The idea of orgies had always been bound up in his thoughts with gluttons: people who ate too much and ate everything put in front of them. There were many such in India. Gluttons developed enormous bellies; orgiasts, in Farquhar's imagination, developed huge and pendulous testicles. Besides, Farquhar was an old man.

When he saw the Turk, he was considerably relieved. Expecting to find some handsome mameluke or even a beautiful Circassian, he saw instead a young man of some twenty-five years, obviously Turkish, but equally obviously, no beauty. He bowed civilly, indicated a chair and, when Farquhar was seated, proceeded to undress him. When it came to his breeches, Farquhar's qualms returned. He stepped back sharply, at which the Turk burst out into a loud and distinctly vulgar laugh. He also shook his head to indicate that Farquhar was mistaken. All the same, he chuckled as he removed his breeches.

Now clad only in his drawers, Farquhar was led to another chamber in which a robe, gleaming with gold lamé, lay on a couch. The Turk helped him into it. Only then did Farquhar notice that at one end of the room, which was furnished and carpeted like any other, was a huge bath of bronze, already filled with steaming water. Into this, from metal flagons, each chased and ornamented, the Turk poured coloured liquids till a heady perfume filled the room. Into this bath Farquhar lowered his lean body and old bones, the Turk turning away.

After some minutes, a languor overcame him, so pleasing he wished he could stay in the bath for ever. Slowly, sleepily, he washed himself with the soft water. But a stable clock chimed in the distance, and the Turk said, in laboured accents, 'Mr. Beckford not like waiting. Please to arise.'

Reluctantly, Farquhar did so and was dried by the Turk, and so relaxed was he by the bath that he did not notice he was naked. The Turk put him back into the lamé robe and led the way back to the first room. Farquhar, who had felt absurd when he first wore it, grubby old man as he was, now swaggered a little.

Lying on the bed of the first room, placed there by some invisible servant, were clothes and jewels such as Farquhar had last seen on the Great Mogul in Delhi. There was a diaphanous shirt, silken trousers embroidered with gold, ornate slippers sewn with pearls, a turban with a jewelled aigret. Having to put on these with the Turk's aid, to Farquhar's delight he found he had to put on a cummerbund. The Turk was about to explain when Farquhar strode to the other end of the room, taking one end of the cummerbund with him. He then pirouetted, the Turk shouting, 'Bravo! Bravo!' The cummerbund emerged perfectly. Farquhar had not felt so happy for a quarter of a century.

The Turk now led Farquhar through the great halls of the Abbey to the place where the staircase of the tower began. Climbing the stairs, Farquhar reflected that Beckford's fancy had taken the form of an Oriental masquerade. Ordinarily such a thing would have displeased Farquhar and made him feel awkward and out of place. But now smelling of the perfumes of the bath, walking through this place which came from a fairy tale, he felt that he would enjoy it. He was, he saw, nostalgic for the East, and must have been for half a lifetime, though never before had he allowed himself to admit it.

He was breathing heavily when he reached the very top of the tower. It was as he expected. There was an Oriental divan strewn with cushions. Persian rugs concealed the walls; carpets from Bokhara covered the floor. Beckford, arrayed like his guest, rose from the divan. The Turk handed his master a silver sprinkler. Farquhar bowed his head. Beckford threw rose water from the sprinkler on his hair. Farquhar gave the elaborate Moslem salute. Beckford responded. He handed back the sprinkler.

' 'Pon my word, Farquhar,' he said, 'how well you do that!'

'Practice, Beckford,' he replied. 'While selling my gunpowder.'

Both men had spoken in their everyday voices, and now they began laughing.

'I am glad,' said Beckford, 'you take my little prank so well. I trust you do not think dressing up absurd.'

'My dear sir,' said Farquhar, as Beckford took his hand and led him to the divan, 'I have had the honour of being invited to dine with the Duke of Wellington. That, sir, was the last time I took a bath until today. I would not have gone, but business is business, and the duke used a great deal of my product. Fifty persons at one table, sir, and as for dressing up, what could be more absurd than generals in full regalia? They clank. I have always thought this Mohammedan dress the most graceful and convenient ever invented.'

Wine and food on silver platters began to be brought in by two servants, each in jackets and baggy breeches, but Farquhar noted ruddy British faces underneath the turbans.

'I was always told, as a boy,' said Beckford, 'that our English way of life was the apex of civilization. But even as a boy I knew it was not true. The Mohammedans, the Persians, the Indians make us look boors. That realization was the beginning of my troubles. But I shall tell you about it later. Now let us eat.'

The meal was made up of pilafs and various vegetables in bowls. Farquhar, before he began to eat, took up a particularly succulent piece of chicken and handed it, in his fingers, to his host. Beckford accepted it. Farquhar was surprised to see that as Beckford ate it, his eyes were filled with tears.

'It was a very dear friend of my boyhood who taught me that custom,' said Beckford. 'Though I believe that I, as the host, should have offered the choicest morsel to you, my guest. It signifies that everything in my house or tent or palace is yours, and the best is at your disposal—as,' said Beckford, 'I hope it soon will be.'

Farquhar replied with a sentence in Urdu. 'That means,' he explained, 'that business should not be mixed with eating; it sours the wine.'

Beckford smiled wryly, and for a while they ate and drank in silence. Then Farquhar said, 'Who was the dear friend of your boyhood who taught you Oriental manners?'

'Cozens,' said Beckford. 'A painter. I have several of his works here in the Eastern Wing. He was a splendid man.'

As the plates were removed and as a servant placed live coals in the cup of hookah to ignite the scented tobacco,

Beckford talked of Cozens, of Iskanderbad, and lastly, of the indecent miniatures.

'I kept them hidden in my bedroom, but they were discovered by an old woman who had been my nurse. I will spare you the commotion, the moralizing and the sermons they caused. It must suffice to say, I was ordered to tear them up, which I did immediately, for I had a deep feeling of guilt. My father came upon me as I was doing this on the terrace. One piece blew away. My father picked it up and looked at it. The tear had greatly emphasized the obscenity, the piece displaying only a large member entering a female. He smiled broadly. Then, seeing my hangdog look, he patted my head. Then he said, "I have company to dine. I want you to dine downstairs. Since you are going to be Prime Minister of England"—for of this my father was quite sure—"you had better know what the English are like." '

The boy had dined and had listened in awe to the conversation of a duke and two earls, together with members of the Cabinet. He had been deeply impressed.

The ladies withdrew, and the port was served. A toast was drunk, and then, to young Beckford's astonishment, his father told a salacious story. He told it badly, but there was a polite guffaw. The duke told another, and very well. Each man in turn told his anecdote, and Beckford, wide-eyed, noted that the incidents described bore a great resemblance to those in the torn-up pictures. Those about sodomites drew a very special laugh.

It was true that a Cabinet minister had once protested as a story began, 'Oh, no, not *that* one in front of the boy!' but Beckford's father thumped the table in his coarse way and roared, 'In front of the boy be damned. Lord Chesterfield himself advised his son that pornography after dinner was the only conversation fit for the perfect gentleman. Go ahead with your story.'

The hubble-bubble sang as the two men drew on the tubes that ran from it.

'And did you learn the lesson that your sensible father was trying to teach you?' said Farquhar. He blew a puff of smoke. 'That the English are hypocrites, I mean.'

'Hypocrisy is not a word in a boy's vocabulary,' said Beckford. 'I was merely bewildered. Nor did I have any time to think. I had confessed that Cozens had given me the pictures. So my mother had his possessions searched. She found a poem addressed unmistakably to me. The sonnet is not an easy form, and Cozens was not a very good poet. It was quite clear he had been making love to me. And from a diary he had kept it was also quite clear he had been making love to the stableboys as well.'

'Why *do* we keep diaries?' said Farquhar.

'Why *do* we make love to stableboys?' asked Beckford in return. 'Oh, there was such a scandal. Cozens was sent packing, and the stableboys were whipped. Nothing was done to me because it was considered to be all Cozens' doing.'

'Was it?'

'Of course not. What did that holy man tell you?'

'Um,' said Farquhar, and puffed. 'Permit me to move the coals on the hookah. It is not drawing well.'

'From then on,' continued Beckford, 'I was thrown much into the company of a girl who was our neighbour.'

'That is what mothers always do. It is a tactic which rarely succeeds.'

'On the contrary, it succeeded admirably. The girl was Lady Margaret Gordon. She later became my wife.'

Farquhar, remembering the chevalier, took the tube from his

mouth and looked curiously at Beckford. 'Ah, yes. You were married, weren't you? Happily, I believe.'

'She was the best wife a sodomite could have,' said Beckford. 'But now let us go out on that little balcony.'

'And,' said Farquhar, 'like the Caliph Vathek, look down on all mankind.'

'Exactly,' said Beckford, and taking his guest's hand in the Oriental manner, he led him to the balcony.

PART THREE

The Women

LADY Margaret Gordon knocked at her aunt's bedroom door. A man's voice bid her enter.

She obeyed and found her aunt seated at her dressing table putting the final touches to a makeup that enamelled her face like that of a porcelain figure.

'Sit down, my dear,' said the enamelled face, 'I shall be finished in a minute.' The voice was so masculine that Lady Margaret thought, as she had thought since childhood, that there must be some invisible ventriloquist behind the window curtains.

She sat, and there was silence, save for the rustle of her aunt's voluminous silks. Lady Margaret looked around the room and saw the portrait of a man who, though young, was already running to fat. It stood on the commode beside the bed, framed in gold. Three small feathers, made up of diamonds, crowned it. Lady Margaret gave the miniature a long look.

Suddenly the man's voice said, 'I see you are looking at my new picture of dear Prinny. And you are thinking, "I can't imagine what the Prince of Wales sees in a plain woman like Auntie Harriet who has a face like an amiable dumpling." How pretty you look when you blush like that, Margaret! And you were such an unprepossessing child. But you needn't blush. Your father said those very words to me more than once and then had the confounded bottom to ask me to ask

75

Prinny to ask the king to get him the Garter. And when he didn't get it, he said, "Swounds ... what's the use of having a sister who's a royal mistress if she can't do a little thing like that!" Margaret, my dear,' went on the deep voice, 'a blush should be a delicate pink. Only the lower orders go crimson.'

Margaret buried her hot cheeks in her hands, then heard her aunt chuckling, exactly as though she were her uncle.

'I'm sorry, my dear,' said her aunt. 'You look so sweet and innocent I could not help teasing you. Besides, you'll be a married woman in a month's time, and you should admit to the family scandal, especially since they are all so proud of it. Come, look up, my dear.'

Margaret obeyed. It was quite true that her aunt had a face like a dumpling and a figure like several put together. But she had quizzical eyes and a kindly mouth, and anyway, she was famous for saying shocking things. Perhaps, thought Margaret, that was what Prinny liked.

Harriet held out a filigree box.

'Here,' she said, 'take one of these bonbons, and I will have one too.'

Aunt and niece chewed silently for a while, Harriet keeping her eyes on the girl.

'How old are you?' asked Harriet, her extraordinary voice thickened by the bonbon, so that now she sounded like a farmer.

Margaret swallowed her sweet and said, 'Eighteen.'

Her aunt chewed, swallowed, sighed and said, 'Your mother was worried because she said that she had to tell you about the duties of a wife, so I offered to do it for her. Your mother is so deeply religious, my dear, that when she talks about what men and women do in bed, she is so shy that every word she says seems to drip with ribald innuendo. Margaret, I want to talk to you about young William Beckford.'

'Yes Aunt.'

'You do like him?'

'Oh, yes, Aunt Harriet. I like him very much, ever since we played together as children. He has such beautiful eyes, such sad eyes, even when he laughs. And I love that faraway look in them when he tells those stories. And I love ....' She stopped. 'Yes Aunt Harriet, I like my future husband.'

'Stories?' said Harriet.

'Wonderful stories, Aunt. About princes and magicians and Baghdad and caverns filled with heaps of diamonds and emeralds guarded by demons and—'

'Did he ever,' said Harriet, interrupting, 'ask you to take down your drawers and show him your bottom?'

Margaret gasped, blushed and then laughed. 'No, Aunt, never. I can't imagine William doing anything of the sort.'

'Neither can I,' said Harriet gloomily. 'That's the trouble.'

Margaret raised her eyebrows. 'Trouble, Aunt Harriet?'

Harriet said nothing. She took up a hand mirror, studied her face for a while, then held it aside.

'Margaret,' she said, 'how much do you know about men?'

'Men?' said Margaret.

'*Men*, you ninny. How do you tell a man from a woman?'

'They wear b-b-breeches,' said Margaret, blushing prettily.

'And have you never been curious about what they have got in those breeches?'

'Oh, yes,' said Margaret brightly.

'Good,' said her aunt. 'Go on.'

'I asked my governess that question when I was ... ooo ... six maybe. She said I should ask my mother.'

'Did you?'

'Yes. "Maman," I said, "what have men got in their breeches?" and she said, "Themselves." I did feel foolish, because I could have thought of that myself, couldn't I?'

Harriet crashed the hand mirror onto the table.

'No!' she roared. 'It takes years of praying on your knees on hassocks to think of an answer like that.'

She furiously dabbed powder on her face till it made a great cloud around her. When it dissipated, she had recovered herself.

'I shall be very, very simple and begin at the very beginning,' she said. 'Did you ever see your brother take a bath?'

'When he was small, yes.'

'Did you notice what he had between his legs. Please, Margaret, do not evade my questions.'

'I won't, Aunt,' said Margaret, and composed her face as though in the schoolroom.

'Well, did you notice it?'

Margaret nodded. 'That little thing, you mean. Yes, I did.'

'It does not remain little,' said Harriet. 'As the boy grows, it grows, it grows.'

Margaret nodded intelligently.

'Have you ever seen one, a man's, I mean?'

Margaret shook her head.

'Well, it's big and it becomes hairy—Margaret, do try not to look so blank.'

Margaret's brows knitted, then cleared.

'I know what you mean,' she said with determined brightness. 'Like a horse's.'

'*Not* like a horse's,' said her aunt, as though she were on a parade ground.

She paused to recover her temper and her breath. When that was done, she said in a lower voice, 'It is perfectly extraordinary how, when you put an English girl across a horse, she can talk of nothing else but horses for years.'

Margaret hung her head.

'I'm sorry, Aunt Harriet,' she said.

'So you should be,' said her aunt. 'I trust you can grasp that this is a most difficult subject for me. We are not at court. God bless the Prince of Wales: he has started a fashion *there* of calling a spade a spade, to say nothing of enjoying a good dig in the garden himself from time to time.'

'My mother says the court is very wicked,' said Margaret.

'Your mother would think a convent of nuns very wicked,' said Harriet. 'Come to think of it, what an excellent abbess she would make. 'Tis a pity she's a Methodist. Where was I?'

'Horses,' said Margaret timidly, 'if I may be so bold.'

Aunt Harriet frowned. 'Ah, yes, I remember.'

'Aunt Harriet,' said Margaret, even more timidly, 'I wasn't really talking about horses. I mean ... what I meant was....' Her voice died away.

'You meant *what*?'

'Foals,' said Margaret.

'Young lady,' said Harriet threateningly, but Margaret plunged on.

'And mares and stallions and ... and ... and ... foals,' she ended lamely. 'Nurse Taylor told me one day.'

'About horses,' said Harriet.

'No, people,' said Margaret in a whisper.

Harriet rose from the dressing table, a mountain of silks snowcapped with her towering wig. She bent over Margaret and kissed her lightly on the forehead.

'I am sorry I shouted at you,' she said. 'It was remiss of me. Prinny says I can be an overbearing old cow when I want to be, though I cannot imagine a cow being overbearing, can you? Mercy,' she said, and swept off to the vast bed, on which she perched, 'how we seem immersed in the animal kingdom. And *that*,' she said, 'is most unsuitable because nothing of that sort goes on among the good creatures.' She paused and eyed her niece.

'What sort?' asked Margaret.

'Buggery,' said her aunt in the loud, clear voice that was so fashionable at court. She rose, and in milder tones she went on, 'If you are going to faint, my dear, I have the smelling salts quite handy.'

She picked up a bottle from the dressing table and turned to face her niece. Margaret was looking at her with calm.

'I'm not going to faint, Aunt Harriet,' she said. 'I know about that.'

'Who told you?'

'Nurse Taylor.'

'What a fount of information that woman must be,' said Harriet.

'You see ...' began Margaret, but then closed her lips.

'Don't be shy,' said her aunt. 'Continue.'

'I'm not being shy,' said Margaret, 'but it's about horses, and you don't like me speaking about them.'

'I don't follow you,' said Harriet, subsiding on her dressing-table stool once more. 'Horses are most respectable in their habits. They would even please your mother if they only wore drawers and breeches.'

'Well, it's more stableboys, really,' said Margaret. 'You see, I've already noticed that William is very, very fond of them.'

'But you also observed that he is not particularly fond of riding,' said Harriet.

'Yes. He prefers driving in his phaeton. Always has. So I asked Nurse Taylor about it—when I knew we were going to be married—and she used that word.'

'Did she explain further?'

'No. She said it was all so shocking.'

'I am disappointed,' said Harriet. 'I was beginning to like that woman. But I suppose she has come under your mother's influence.'

'But you're not shocked with buggery,' said Margaret, pronouncing the word with innocence.

'At the Court of St. James's,' said her aunt with pride, 'it is most unfashionable to be shocked.'

'Oh, goody!' said Margaret, clapping her hands. 'Then you can tell me what buggery is.'

Aunt Harriet got up and took a majestic turn around her bedroom. She finished up facing her niece.

'I shall begin with God,' she said decisively.

Margaret nodded piously. 'Everything comes from God,' she said.

'Yes, doesn't it?' said her aunt. 'It really is most extraordinary. Well, my dear, your mother has doubtless told you numberless times. "Male and female created He them".'

Margaret nodded.

'So far so good,' said her aunt, 'but then, Margaret, he went on tinkering. He made men who did not love women but who loved other men and—to come down to the subject in hand—boys.'

'And William loves boys?' said Margaret.

'He does.'

'Well,' said Margaret, 'I think that is beautiful. I think it is very Christian. My mother says we should love *everybody*.'

'Unfortunately loving everybody on this realm is punishable by hanging by the neck until you are dead. Especially when everybody includes underage boys.'

Neither spoke for a while. Then Margaret straightened her back in her chair.

'My mother,' she said firmly, 'would never betroth me to a man who might be hanged like a common criminal.'

'Beckford can never be a *common* criminal,' said Harriet. 'He has an income of one hundred thousand pounds a year. I would like to be able to say that you cannot hang a hundred thousand pounds a year, but we English are unpredictable. We cut off the head of Charles the First who had rather more. You see, it all depends on who gets the money when the deed is done. In that case, it was Cromwell.'

'But if William were hanged, it would be me who— Oh, no, it does not bear thinking of,' said Margaret.

'Yes, my dear, you would be the richest woman in England. My dear Prinny said it himself.'

'You don't mean that William's ... William's *boys* ... are discussed at St. James's,' said Margaret.

'My dear girl, to discuss such things is almost a constitutional duty of the heir of the throne in England. One of the reasons why King Charles lost his head was that he had already lost it over a pretty youth called Villiers. *Of course* the Prince of Wales discussed it with me. I am, after all, your aunt. He was most reasonable. To tell you the truth, I didn't put it beyond your mother to have thought of the fact that you would be the heiress of a man who risked his life every time he saw a quiff of hair and a pair of well-fitting breeches. These women who think deeply about the world to come often take a chillingly level view of life here below. But Prinny said, "No, she was cleverer than that".'

'Aunt Harriet,' said Margaret, her fingers clenched tightly together on her lap, 'this conversation is causing me great distress, and I do not think I should continue it.'

'Then I shall ring for a dish of tea,' said Harriet, and did so, with a regal gesture. Nothing was said while the tea was ordered, carried in, prepared by Harriet, and a cup of it was drunk.

When this was done, Harriet said, 'Margaret, dear girl, do you know who Shakespeare was?'

'Yes, Aunt,' said Margaret eagerly, glad that the conversation was to be changed. 'My tutor told me. He was a poet who wrote plays. His verses are incorrect.'

'Quite wilfully so,' agreed her aunt. 'He had talent but no ear for numbers. But he wrote some lines about England that Prinny likes to quote. You see, he sometimes wakes up in the middle of the night, thinking about his future. And *I* have to wake up, too, of course. He says these lines by Shakespeare about England. Prinny hates the place, but he thinks he ought not to, since he'll be its king one day. Why he chooses Shakespeare I don't know unless it's because of his father. The king can't stand the man, so naturally Prinny reads him. Well, one of these lines calls England "This precious stone set in a silver sea." Well, Prinny was saying this at three in the morning—he was still pretty drunk—when *I* said, "So that's what her game is," meaning your mother. More tea, my dear?'

Margaret, quite put off her guard by this rambling speech, incautiously said, 'What game?'

'What will really happen if your future husband is caught with a boy? Somebody—somebody who has need, say, for a few thousand pounds—will warn him. For a trifling expense, Beckford hires a boat and lands at Calais. He is then perfectly safe. They do not hang men for loving boys on the Continent.'

'Why, Aunt?'

'Religion,' said Harriet in her deepest voice. 'They are mostly Catholics, and if they did hang people for loving boys, they would have had to hang more than one Pope, which would never do. You do see the drift of my remarks, don't you? England is an island. Beckford puts the English Channel between him and that island, and he is safe. You stay behind, and Beckford gives you a handsome slice of that hundred thousand a year.'

Margaret got up, putting down her saucer and cup with a rattle.

'Do you mean to say that my mother ... *my mother* ... thought up this ... this nefarious plan?'

'No,' said Harriet, indistinctly because she was munching a biscuit. 'Your saintly mother got to her knees and prayed for guidance.' She swallowed the biscuit. 'And she got it,' Harriet concluded. Then she said, 'Sit down, my dear.'

'I will not sit down,' Margaret replied, 'and let me tell you that, what's more, I would not stay behind in England if poor William had to flee. I would go with him.'

Harriet studied the tears which were now shining in Margaret's eyes.

'You love him, don't you?' she said.

Margaret nodded. 'For years,' she said.

'Then marry him,' said her aunt. 'Don't leave him, but *do* sit down and listen to me. I have something to say, and I am worth listening to. I am not the mistress of the heir to the throne for nothing.'

Margaret stood still. She gazed at her aunt.

'You did say I loved William, didn't you?'

'Yes, my dear. You love him very much.'

'Nobody else has said that to me. Nobody in spite of all the river of words they've said about the wedding, the settlement, the home we'll live in. Nobody ever said, "You love William". So I'll listen to you, Aunt Harriet.'

'Then dry your eyes, and I'll ring for the servant to carry away the tray.'

When this was done, in slow state, Harriet said, 'I am now going to tell you how to be a good wife to a husband who loves boys. The first thing you must remember is that husbands are not faithful. They keep mistresses. *I* am one. Mistresses are very annoying to wives; I mean the thought of them. They say to themselves, "What can my husband see in that dreadful woman?" and then they set themselves, the ninnies, to copy the mistress. Prinny is married, and you should just see how his wife tries to imitate *my* wit, *my* poise, *my* elegance, *my* knowledge of the world. Now William Beckford will never have a mistress. Why? Because he has you. He has to have you for the sake of peace and quiet. But for a man who loves boys, one woman is enough—quite enough.'

'But do you mean I shall have to share my husband with a ... a ... stableboy?'

'Better a stableboy than another woman. A stableboy won't drop nasty observations in your husband's ear about the way you are losing your figure. A stableboy won't sweep into one of your receptions and give you a knowing look as he flutters his fan. A stableboy won't want a set of earrings every time your husband gives *you* earrings. A stableboy won't want a coach and a brace of expensive horses to go driving round the park. Think how silly he would look.'

Margaret laughed at the vision. Then she said, with practicality in her tone, 'But what sort of presents will William make?'

'Boys need very little. Some clothes, but not too expensive, or they will arouse suspicions. Pocket money, but not too much for the same reason.'

'So it's an expensive vice,' said Margaret.

'Not quite as cheap as it might appear,' said her aunt. 'Your mother is very kind to a number of poor families, I believe?'

'Oh, yes. It's part of her duty as a Christian. Mine too.'

'It will be part of Beckford's *urgent* duty to be very kind to certain families,' said Harriet. 'But whereas your mother does her duty with a trumpet being blown before her like the Pharisee in the Bible, Beckford will do good by stealth, as Our Lord recommended. How many families does your mother support?'

'About twenty.'

'I hope Beckford doesn't have as many. It will be bad for his health. But he will have two or three or four, and he will have to see each member of it through life from the cradle to the grave.'

'But how can a father let his son be corrupted for the sake of money?' asked Margaret in genuine wonder.

'He will *not* let his son be corrupted, my dear. On the contrary, he will insist that his son marry and raise children. Beckford will pay for the marriage and for the children and for a house in which they can all grow up. The beloveds of all the pederasts I have known have all ended up in the most suffocating state of married respectability.'

'Peder . . .' said Margaret, frowning. 'I haven't heard that word before.'

'Pederast,' repeated Harriet obligingly. 'Pederast, the one who does it. "Pederasty", the thing he does. I recommend the word to you. People like your future husband are commonly known as buggers and sodomites. The first word is derived from a sect of Bulgarian Christians considered by several Popes to be heretics. "Sodomite", as I need not tell you, derives from a town named in the Bible, destroyed by Jehovah. Both names, you will note, have religious overtones. "Pederast" is merely the Greek for boy lover. The fact, you note, *tout court*, with no theological overtones. Which reminds me to tell you that Beckford will insist on telling you to the point of boredom that the Greeks did not disapprove of pederasty. This is not true. It was accepted in the highest strata of society, but that is all. But since I have known the Court of St. James's, I begin to wonder if there is anything which is *not* accepted in the highest strata of society.'

'Are there peder . . . pederasts at court?'

'Several, my dear. Remind me to give you a list of their names.'

'Why?'

'Because you must warn your husband of them. They will be his worst enemies.'

'How *can* I warn him, Aunt Harriet. I can't very well talk about the subject, can I?'

'My dear Margaret, the heaviest cross you will have to bear in your married life is that he will never stop talking about the subject to *you*.'

'You mean in so many words?' said Margaret with alarm.

'Not in the first year of marriage. But if he starts talking about our glorious victories on the Continent, it means he's fallen in love with a soldier. If he deplores the state of our naval establishments, he's lost his heart to a midshipman. And if he bores you with theories about the rotation of crops, it's a ploughboy. It is curious, but all three professions have a compelling attraction for pederasts.'

'Really, Aunt, is that so? I am learning so much, and I'm sure I'm very grateful. But can you explain why gentlemen should be attracted to such vulgar people?'

'No, I cannot,' said her aunt, 'and I am not going to try. I have never in my life met a refined footman, but it is remarkable what an effect they have on *our* sex, my dear.'

Margaret giggled.

'How right you are, Aunt,' she said. 'And wicked.'

'Why did you giggle, you minx?'

'Because when I was twelve, I fell romantically in love with a footman called Thomas. He had blue eyes and chestnut curls. My mother noticed the languishing looks I gave him, and she sent him away.'

'Have you been in love with a footman since?'

'Of course not. I was just a little girl then.'

'And there you have the nub of the whole matter. Beckford will always be a little boy of twelve.'

'But he's the most grown-up, well-read, sophisticated man I know. Everybody says he's much older than his age.'

'Pederasts very often are sophisticated. Prinny says they are the only members of his entourage who have any manners or conversation. He always has a brace or two of them about when he entertains the French ambassador. But it is a mask, my dear. They are all little boys at heart. That is why they seek out other little boys.'

'But I can't go around thinking of my husband as a little boy.'

'What wife thinks of her husband as anything else?'

Margaret looked thoughtful.

'Yes, you are very clever. My mother told me that.'

'What else did she tell you about your duties as a wife? But come,' she said, rising and going to a cabinet, 'you must take a small glass of this excellent cordial with me.'

'No, thank you, Aunt. I never drink.'

'Then I shall,' said Harriet, and tossed back a tiny glass of green fluid. 'Ha!' she said, with satisfaction. 'What else did she tell you?'

'I must have children.'

Harriet nodded as she resumed her seat. 'Because God said to Adam and Eve, "Be fruitful and multiply." Fruitful,' she said. 'Such an ugly word. Besides, I should have thought that fruit was a most ill-chosen subject considering the circumstances. But don't let me interrupt. A glass of cordial makes me chatter.'

'She said I must always see that my husband is comfortable. "The way to a man's heart is through his belly," she told me.'

'William Beckford has, at the early age of twenty, no less

than four cooks that he even takes travelling with him. If you mean to capture his heart through his abdomen, you are going to have some pretty powerful rivals.'

'I suppose Mother didn't think of that. Our cook is appalling.'

'What else did your mother tell you?'

'She told me I must keep my husband happy.'

'Did she tell you how you should keep one of the richest young men in England happy?'

'She says money isn't important. She says Our Lord taught that it was easier for a camel to go through the eye of a needle than for a rich man to enter the kingdom of heaven.'

'That was a remark made by a man who had no private income to a number of other men who had no private incomes either. Beckford has one hundred thousand pounds a year. Men like that might have difficulties with St. Peter, a poor man all his life and no doubt prejudiced in the matter. But I assure you they have few difficulties while they are on earth. I know. My dear, you are young to face the same problem as I did when Prinny fell in love with me. After all, what could I do for a man who was Prince of Wales and would one day be king? I could make him happy in bed to the best of my ability. But we women are all much the same shape, and, if I do not shock your young ears, while there are a great number of ways of making love, men as a rule like only a couple of them and are rarely at their best when faced with the unusual. Besides, I would be at the mercy of every expert courtesan in the kingdom. I could not flatter him; he had duchesses ready to do that. I could not make him comfortable as a woman should her lover; he had an array of servants to do that. What then, I wondered, *could* I do?'

She picked up her hand mirror and examined her face in it.

'As I remarked before, Margaret,' she said, 'you've often wondered why the Prince of Wales could fall in love with a woman who has a face like mine.'

'Oh, *no*,' said Margaret.

'When you are telling lies, my dear, you seem just like your mother. Margaret, I am plain. Even the portraits that Prinny has had painted of me are plain. I once said so to Prinny, and he replied, "That is because they look like you, but they cannot talk like you." I was so surprised to hear Prinny make an epigram that I kissed him in front of the painter. But Prinny was right. He loves me because I talk to him. Not just chatter or gossip or endearments. You see, I had found out something about him. Listen carefully, Margaret.

'I discovered that Prinny,' she went on, 'loved talking about politics. But nobody would listen to him. That was because, in the first place, he knew nothing about politics whatever, so when he talked about them he talked like Poor Poll. In the second place, he couldn't learn about them because his father, the king, wouldn't let him. Kings prefer their sons to be fools, especially about ruling the country. Of course, Prinny *will* rule the country. But he will do it very badly. Then people will say, "It's not like the golden days under his father," and that, of course, is just what his father wants. So what did I do? I studied politics. I talked to politicians, and then I let Prinny talk his head off to me. I listened to him with awe and admiration. People will listen to him with awe and admiration when he becomes George the Fourth, and I daresay he will talk the same muddle and nonsense. But I listen to him *now*, and he loves me for it. Just so, you must listen to Beckford when he wants to talk about something he can discuss with nobody else.'

'What is that?' said Margaret, but caught herself up. 'Oh, yes, I see. *Boys*.'

'Exactly.'

'I know nothing about them—not those sort of boys.'

'Those sort of men will tell you. Margaret, you must cultivate the company of pederasts as I did that of politicians. You will have the advantage that pederasts wash more frequently than Members of Parliament. You will approve of their vices, and if you don't know what they are, you must persuade them to tell you, and you must never be shocked. You must call it the Italian Vice and talk about the boys that Michelangelo painted for the popes to say mass under. Have you seen the Sistine, my dear? No? I have. It is most amusing. His Holiness looks straight up at their groins as he dances about in that peculiar ritual. Well, learn all you can, and let Beckford talk all he wants to. Particularly in bed. That will be his most awkward moment. Encourage him to tell you about his loves before he blows out the candle. Or better still, when the candles are blown out.... You seem distraught, Margaret. Are you listening to me?'

Margaret nodded. 'Oh, yes, Aunt. It's just that I think I've seen the way I can do it. William loves telling stories—about caliphs and Baghdad and things like that. I'm sure he sees himself as one—caliph, I mean. So, you see, the Caliph loves boys, and Beckford will tell me all about it. And I'll know he's talking about himself, and ... and we'll *both* know.'

Harriet rose. She went over to Margaret and taking her niece's chin, tilted it upward, and said, 'You will make an excellent wife.' Then she stood back and looked thoughtfully at her niece.

'Do you know William Courtenay?' she said.

'No. Who is he?'

'A schoolboy.' Harriet's face grew suddenly grave. 'You will hear a great deal about him when you are married. Stand by Beckford, Margaret, when the storm breaks.'

William Beckford leaned upon the balustrade of his tower. Farquhar, a little dizzy with looking down upon men as ants, sat gratefully on a small stone seat.

'As for my wife,' said Beckford, 'we married very hastily. All the same it was a very grand wedding. One of her aunts brought half the Court of St. James's, and the Prince of Wales sent a gift—a great brass jar of Benares ware, all finely chased and standing five feet high. It was in perfect taste and made up for the monstrous objects that Margaret's family sent. Her aunt told me that Prinny had chosen it himself. How strange to have a man of taste on the throne! I am told he is eating his heart out to come and see this Abbey, but the depraved old lecher is afraid of meeting me.'

'His Majesty King George the Fourth,' said Farquhar, 'is drunk by ten o'clock and dead drunk by three. But he has, as you say, good taste in everything—except himself.'

'We were the talk of London. I was a brand snatched from the burning, and only just in time. I had been exceedingly foolish. I was deeply in love with a schoolboy who greatly resembled me when I, too, was a boy. I could not bear to be without his company, and when he was sent away to St. Paul's School, I was desolate. I went to see him. He led me to an empty classroom, and we kissed. We were, of course, seen. Boys are very beautiful; they have the most shapely bottoms, but they have the filthiest of minds and no more moral restraint than pirates. The boy who had seen us immediately told his friends and, under very little compulsion, the head-master. The news that the most eligible bachelor in the land had been caught with his hand in a schoolboy's breeches—or so the monstrous little spy had said—rocked the town. Men who were head over heels in debt gloated; mothers with marriageable daughters were enraged. The Prince of Wales told Margaret's aunt that the young pup should get married, and married I was. Come, let us go inside. The sun is getting behind the trees, and there'll soon be a rather nasty damp mist.'

They went inside and descended the tower. Still in their Oriental robes, the two men sat in one of the vast Gothic halls. Candelabra had already been lit but dispelled the gloom only in small islands of light.

'There is nothing incongruous about our sitting under these Gothic arches in this costume, for after all, the Mohammedans invented them,' said Beckford.

Farquhar gazed upward but could see nothing.

'The Mohammedans have great talents,' he said. 'They can make love to their boys and still satisfy their numberless women. I admire that. I have never married because I was afraid I would not be able to give my wife what she had a right to demand.'

'I detect, Mr. Farquhar, a note of moral superiority in that remark.'

Farquhar laughed. 'But sodomites often are very strict moralists, in their own way,' he said. 'I suppose you were a good Mohammedan, and all went well.'

'I was not only afraid I could not make love to my wife, I had a downright horror of the whole idea. My friends pointed out that she had a boy's bottom, as she had in a way, but the more I thought of that, the more I saw it might lead me into even deeper trouble. But if I was afraid of a woman in bed, I was much more afraid of one other thing. So I plunged into marriage.'

'What was that other thing?'

'The English,' said Beckford, 'when they are being respectable. Sometimes I walk this hall until dawn because I have had a nightmare and dare not go back to sleep again.'

In the candlelight Farquhar saw Beckford's face grow strained. Globules of sweat were on his upper lip. His body was rigid.

'I am in a cart in a London street. A crowd—but no. It is most ill-mannered to tell one's dreams. Instead, I shall give the reality.'

He got up and left the hall. When he came back, he had removed his turban and had an album in his hands.

He sat down. He moved a candlestick nearer to him and opened the book. Farquhar saw that a news sheet had been pasted onto one of the pages.

'You will have heard of the Vere Street scandal,' Beckford said.

'I have heard it mentioned. But I was away in Europe at the time, and I know very little about it.'

'Vere Street is in London, and in it was a house—a lodgings—for sodomites. It was a sort of club where men could meet boys, and there were rooms for enjoying them. It was, if you like, a brothel, but not one run for gain. In fact, the frequenters were sentimentalists. They had a chapel in which they celebrated weddings. One that came to light was between a six-foot guardsman and a little dancing master.'

Beckford, who had recovered his poise, smiled, and so did Farquhar.

'Yes, indeed, it is laughable,' said Beckford. 'Nothing else in the story is. The club was discovered. The club members were arrested. Here is the account of what happened. Seven men were put on trial. Here are their names: William Amos, James Cook, Philip Kett, William Thompson, Richard Francis, James Done and Robert Aspinall. The date was September the second, eighteen hundred and ten. With them were some of the boys and men who were their amours.'

Beckford bent and read: ' "Miss Selina, a police runner, the Duchess of Devonshire, a blacksmith's apprentice, Leonara, a drummer boy, and Miss Sweetlips as he was called, a grocer's delivery boy. The seven men were found guilty and sentenced to three years' imprisonment and to stand in the pillory in the Haymarket, opposite Panton Street." '

Beckford continued to read, throwing the correct emotion into his voice to match the words of the broadside.

' "The disgust felt by all ranks of society at the detestable conduct of these wretches occasioned many thousands to become spectators of their punishment. The shops from Ludgate Hill to the Haymarket were shut up, and the streets lined with people, waiting to see the offenders pass." '

'Nothing but a surge of lust in his loins would persuade a Londoner to shut up his shop on a weekday,' said Farquhar.

'There are Englishmen who will not allow even that to make them depart from their principles,' replied Beckford. 'Listen to this: "Shortly after twelve a number of carts were driven by butchers' boys, who had previously taken care to fill them with offal, dung and so forth appertaining to their several slaughterhouses. A number of hucksters...." ' Beckford paused and repeated the last word. ' "Hucksters were also put into requisition, who carried on their heads baskets of apples, together with the remains of divers dogs and cats. The whole were sold to the populace at a high price, who spared no expense to provide themselves with the necessary articles of assault." '

'The English equivalent,' said Farquhar, 'of the paper confetti they sell abroad at carnival time.'

'Just so,' said Beckford. 'Well, the poor devils were placed in a cart and drawn through the streets. Let me read you a little more of this excellent prose so that you will know what happened.'

He resumed reading. ' "The first salute received by the offenders was a volley of mud, and a serenade of hisses, hooting and execration, which compelled them to fall flat on their faces in the cart. The shower of mud continued during their passage to the Haymarket. Before they reached halfway to the scene of their exposure, they were not discernible as human beings. They resembled bears dipped in a stagnant pool. Before any of them reached the place of punishment, their faces were disfigured by blows and mud; before they mounted, their whole persons appeared one heap of filth."

'They are now in the pillory or apparently pillories. The writer's masterly description fails him a little in this matter. But he goes on: "Upwards of fifty women were permitted to stand in a ring, who assailed them incessantly with mud, dead cats, rotten eggs, potatoes and buckets filled with mud, offal and dung. After an hour they were taken back along the route by which they had come and received similar salutes. When they were taken from the pillory, the butchers' men and the women, who had been so active, were plentifully regaled with gin and beer, procured from a subscription made on the spot." '

Beckford paused. 'There is a final touch,' he said, and read. ' "On the way back they were chained and placed in such a manner that they could not lie down in the cart." '

'The spectators,' said Farquhar, 'must have protested at the bad stage management of the first part of the show. I trust that the poor wretches survived.'

' "Some," ' said Beckford, ' "were cut in the head with brickbats and bled profusely." '

He closed the book.

'And now you know why, when I was told to marry, I married. I was, after all, only a boy of twenty. Now that you have obliged my fancy graciously, let us take off these clothes, and remember we are not in Baghdad, or indeed Venice or Paris, but in England. It is a dangerous thing to forget too long.'

PART FOUR

The Pillory

As the wedding day had approached, Harriet had grown more explicit in her advice and the bride-to-be less blushing when she heard it. One day Harriet had swept into the house, kissed Margaret and said, 'I have great news for you.' With that she carried her off to a temple, artfully ruined, that Beckford's father had built. Shutters had incongruously been fitted across the cella behind the columns because of the English climate.

Harriet had closed the shutters with care. There was a Roman copy of a Greek statue against the back wall of the enclosure. Harriet unpinned a rose she wore in her bosom and laid it ceremoniously at the feet of the statue.

Margaret said, 'How delightful. A pagan rite. How shocked Mama would be. She is always wanting the idol as she calls it to be taken away.'

'It is the god Aesculapius,' said Harriet, 'the god of healing. I have made him a small oblation because what I have to say is decidedly medical in tone. My dear girl, I am happy to tell you that your future husband is not impotent. Do you know what that means?'

'Yes, Aunt. I looked it up once. It means a man who cannot have babies.'

'In certain circumstances I could mention that would be a useful gift in a man. It means much more.'

On either side of the cella, again with little regard to historical accuracy, were two nude statues on plinths. One of these, an Apollo, had its genitals covered with a fig leaf. But this, being of plaster, had partly crumbled away. Harriet tapped the statue in its groin, dislodging another fragment of plaster.

'Impotence in a man means that he cannot raise *this* at the apposite moment. It remains as this sculptor has carved it. It is popularly believed that pederasts are afflicted with this drawback. Beckford is not. He is not of Herculean proportions, but neither is he skimpy.'

'But, Aunt Harriet, how can you *know*?'

'I got it from the horse's mouth. Who should know better than the boy?'

'Courtenay?'

'The same. I gave him a day in town.'

'But he is only a little boy. How could he....'

'He is a fifteen-year-old schoolboy at St. Paul's School, a sink of iniquity only surpassed by Eton College. He is exceedingly popular with his school-fellows, and since he is far from robust—nay, he is delicate—I concluded that he had a dirty mind. So it turned out. Besides, what more could a boy ask than to be whisked into town by a notorious woman of the world? He told me all after one bottle of claret.'

'Then my William *can* have babies?' said Margaret, clapping hands.

'Do not jump to conclusions, my girl,' said Harriet severely. 'Let us proceed step by step.'

'But I *want* babies!' said Margaret, stamping her foot.

'Step by *step*,' repeated Harriet. 'As Aesculapius there will confirm, yes, Beckford can have babies, provided, however, he can have them with William Courtenay.'

'What a disgusting idea!'

'And so full of difficulties that not even the Greeks,' said

Harriet waving a hand at the ruins, 'could include it in their stories of the gods. No, to have a baby, Beckford must make love to you in the accepted manner. To which suggestion, Beckford will reply in your own words: "What a disgusting idea!"'

'Aunt Harriet,' said Margaret, 'if you say any more things like that, I shall burst into tears.'

Her aunt walked majestically across the enclosure and examined one of the statues.

Margaret, nettled that her threat of weeping had so little effect, said, somewhat sharply, 'Please remember, Aunt, that I have not had the privilege of frequenting the Court of St. James's, nor had the privilege of the conversation of its highest ornament. I am a simple girl, brought up in the country.'

'Then God help you,' said Harriet, in a most matter-of-fact way. She continued her examination of the statue.

There was silence in the ruin for a while. Margaret seated herself on a fallen block and stared at the wall. At length she said, in a small voice, 'I see what you mean, Aunt. Please go on. Please help me.'

Harriet turned away from the statue towards her niece.

'I really think,' she said, 'that every bit of that statue is a fake. The Italians turn them out by the dozen. "For the English," they say.' She paused. 'Yes, my dear, I will help you. Listen, and I shall tell you what to do.'

She crossed the cella and sat beside her on the marble block.

'In the first place you must insist that he sleeps with you and in your marriage bed. You can tell him he can make the bed as big as a bowling green if he wants, but he must sleep in it. Not for the sake of your conjugal rights, but for the sake of his precious neck. If he sleeps alone, the servants will spread the news, and it will be all over London. A wit at court has already suggested that he and his friends send wedding presents to St. Paul's School addressed to Courtenay. The bed, then, and Beckford in it, perforce. Now nights are long, and men are at their most potent—when, that is, they have not made love the night before—they are most potent in the early hours of the morning. All that time their minds are not very active, but their bodies are. Beckford is a man of considerable fantasy. If you can persuade him you are a boy, he will make love to you.'

'In heaven's name,' exclaimed Margaret, 'what do you expect me to do? Learn to whistle?'

'No, my dear. Just lie still. Do not use perfume; do not paint your lips. Do not insist on kisses. Lie with your head on his shoulder like a boy sleeping with his elder brother. That, you see, is the way William Courtenay does it. I found it *most* attractive when I made love to him.'

Margaret rose. 'Aunt Harriet! Do you mean to tell me—'

'He is fifteen, and as pretty as a picture,' said Harriet with simplicity. 'One of the things that relieves the boredom of royal courts is that they are filled with pretty pageboys. Come, my dear, it is time we returned to the house.'

The gloom of the taproom of the King's Arms was a little relieved by the uniform of the man and boy—the man in the red breeches and splendidly laced livery of Lord Loughborough, the boy in the much bebuttoned uniform of a drummer in the Grenadiers.

The boy slapped the man on his broad shoulders, raising his arm to reach them.

'And how's Keyhole Charley today?' he asked brightly.

'Mr. Charles Foxley to you, you cheeky monkey,' answered the man. Man and boy sat down at a worn table. The man took off his powdered wig, threw it on the table and set about scratching his cropped hair. With his wig he had the blank face of a footman. Without it he became a youngish man with something of the looks and snub nose of a sentimental curate.

'How's the feet?' asked the boy whose nose was also snub, as befitted a drummer boy, as did everything else in his features from his pink cheeks to his oversized ears.

'None the better for your asking,' said the footman.

'Christ, we're crosspatch today,' said the boy. Then, raising his voice, he said to the potboy, who was leaning against the wall, 'Two pints of ale, boy, and hurry.'

The potboy made no move. The drummer, with an elaborate gesture, threw a silver shilling on the table. Immediately, the potboy darted off.

'Where d'you get that money?' asked the footman.

'I got it in the usual way,' said the boy. 'A hundred lashes well laid on. Good man, the lieutenant. Appreciates good work. Always picks me to do a flogging and tips me.'

An expression of deep pain settled on Charles' face.

'I can see blood on that piece of silver,' he said in solemn tones.

'No, you can't,' said the boy. 'I didn't get it till they'd untied the bugger and carried 'im orf.'

The footman sadly shook his head.

'You'll say orders is orders,' he said. 'But *I* say fancy making an innocent boy whip a poor soldier—and for money.'

'I don't do it for money. I do it for fun,' said the boy, at which point the potboy brought two tankards of ale, scooped up the shilling and gave the drummer a handful of copper change.

Charles looked into his ale.

'I don't think I can touch it,' he said. 'I don't really.'

'Oh, go on,' said the boy easily. 'It's like what the chaplain says, "What's a flogging?" he says. "A few blows and a few oh's." '

The footman took hold of the handle of his tankard.

'It's a cruel and wicked world we live in,' he said. 'But a day will come when the wickedness will pass away, and men will love one another like brothers.' He raised his tankard. 'I drink to the New Jerusalem,' he said.

'Wot they done with the old one?' asked the boy.

'You shut your gob,' said the footman. He buried his nose in the tankard and was about to drink when the boy said in well-feigned alarm, 'Look *out*, Charley, I can see blood in it.'

Foam flew in all directions as Charley spluttered and choked. He took some time to recover his breath.

'Beer all over me cuff,' he mourned. 'I wouldn't mind taking a whip to *your* backside,' he said as he dried himself, and the drummer boy rolled in his seat with laughter.

'You may laugh,' said Foxley, 'but I've got a bit of news that'll make you laugh on the other side of your face.'

But the news was postponed by the arrival of a small man, soberly but expensively dressed, his hands encased in embroidered gloves and a fine lace stock at his throat. He sat down at the table without invitation.

' 'Lo, Mr. Limper,' said the drummer boy, in a respectful voice. 'Buy you a drink, Mr. Limper?'

Limper regarded him with bright, piercing eyes that shone on either side of a sharp nose springing from spectacularly sunken cheeks.

'Been at it again?' said Limper.

'Yes.'

'You might have told me,' said Limper. 'I got someone who'll pay your sergeant a guinea to watch one of you boys at it. Make it brandy.'

'A guinea?' said the boy. 'But how's it to be done?'

'From a window, you blockhead, like the others do it. But

mind you,' said Limper, 'my client's got to have a good clear view of the flogging.'

'Who is he?'

'How do you know it isn't a she?' asked Limper.

'If it is,' said the boy with a shrewd air, 'she'd have to dress as a man.'

'Who are you to make terms?' said Mr. Limper. 'You tell your sergeant.'

'Right,' said the drummer boy. He ordered the brandy, watched silently while it was served, then said to Foxley, 'What was that news?'

Foxley did not answer at once. Instead, he gazed from Limper to the boy and back again in a dramatic manner.

'Pimps and perverts,' he said, shaking his head. 'But it'll pass. The glorious dawn is on its way, when men will live in fraternity and liberty. I drink,' he said, raising his tankard, 'to the American rebels, God bless 'em.'

The boy shuddered. 'Don't talk of it,' he said. 'If the rebels don't shoot the arse off you, the Indians take the skin off your skull, hair and all.'

Limper sipped his brandy. 'Ah, America,' he said, admiringly. 'What a market! A trollop on the frontier is worth her weight in gold. But will any of my girls go? No! This nation's got no guts left. No wonder the rebels are beating the breeches off us. By the way, talking of politics, I dropped in to tell you, Tom, your fancy man's in trouble.'

'Who?' said the boy, alarmed. 'You don't mean Full-Bottom?'

'I do.'

'He does,' agreed Foxley, in a hurt tone. 'And I'd have told you first if you'd let me get a word in edgeways. The things I heard this afternoon....'

'Trust Keyhole Charley,' said the boy, derisively.

'I didn't listen to no keyhole,' said Foxley, with dignity. 'The library door was ajar. And,' he rushed on, lest once more the word be taken from him, 'I heard his lordship say to that solicitor fellow who's always hanging around, I heard him say, "We've got Thurlow by the balls, Harry, if he's got any, which I very much doubt. He's a pouf, Harry, a prancing pouf. Do you know what, Harry? That goddamned sodomite Beckford has had the infernal gall to ask for a peerage, and Thurlow, swishing his backside, has been fool enough to ask the king to give him one. We've got him, Harry. I'm going to spread the whole vile thing in every news sheet in town." That's what me lord said, word for word.'

The news was greeted in silence. Then Limper said to the boy, 'You know Beckford, don't you?'

'The Sultana? Yes.' He bit his lip.

'And you know Thurlow, too,' said Foxley, reprovingly.

'We don't do anything dirty,' said the boy, defensively.

'Oh, no,' said Foxley with heavy sarcasm. 'Oh, dear me, no.'

'He whips him,' said the pimp, as though glossing a text. 'And you can't be hanged for that. But it's nasty. Your master Loughborough is a man who doesn't do things by halves. Before he's done, we'll all have our good names dragged through the mud. What a blazing fool that Beckford must be.'

At that moment Full-Bottom was sitting gravely on a very large red cushion, listening to his peers debate that very subject which had engaged the three companions in the King's Arms: America. The nickname was apt, since Lord Thurlow was the Lord Chancellor of England and, as such, sat on the woolsack wearing a full-bottomed wig. Dressed in his black and gold robes, Thurlow did not look like a pouf, nor, when, the sitting over, he rose and walked processionally behind the mace, did he sway his hips. Indeed, he seemed fittingly to uphold the dignity of Parliament. An amiable man, he had no enemies, except Foxley's employer. Lord Loughborough hated him, with a burning, permanent hate for one good reason, and one only: Loughborough wanted to be lord chancellor, and with the aid of Beckford's folly, in due course, he was.

Later that night the lord chancellor of England dismissed his carriage at Temple Bar, telling his coachmen to return at midnight. Pulling his hat well forward over his eyes, he plunged into the narrow lanes that lay between the Fleet and the Thames. He came to a bleak and battered house and, noting with pleasure that the windows were lit, took out a key and let himself in. He entered a room which contained only a large wardrobe and some hooks in the wall. Working quickly, he took off all his clothes. He opened the wardrobe filled with uniforms. Selecting one, he put it on, having much difficulty with the buttons because his fingers were trembling. When he had finally pulled on the regulation boots, he stood arrayed as a corporal of the Grenadiers. He coughed loudly.

'Wait,' said a stern voice from the other room, and Lord Chancellor Thurlow waited, though with some impatience. He hoped the wait would not be too long, but five minutes passed in silence, and the lord chancellor realized, with a sinking heart, that he was thinking, *worrying*, about the Treaty of Paris which had given the American rebels all they wanted, to the shame, he thought, of his countrymen.

But just as gloom was about to envelop him, a sharp voice from the other room said, 'Corporal Full-Bottom! Forward march!'

Relieved, the lord chancellor straightened his shoulders, pulled in his stomach and marched into the other room, stamp-

ing his feet. The next room was a little more furnished than
the other, but not much. There was a deal table, a chair and
nothing else save a tripod of wood, some seven feet high, such
as was used for flogging in the Army. At the table sat a
uniformed figure wearing the insignia of a captain of the
Grenadiers. By the triangle stood Tom, the drummer boy,
idly swinging a cat-o'-nine-tails. The lord chancellor shivered
agreeably, then stood rigidly to attention. The captain was
bent over a piece of paper.

The captain looked up.

'Corporal Full-Bottom!' he said in admirably harsh military
tones. His face was not, however, at all military, being fat and
jowled with an amiable expression and lips which were
struggling with a grin. The chancellor noted, as always, this
unmartial face and looked above it at the wall. The face could
not be helped since it belonged, not to a grenadier, but a
barrister with a rapidly expanding practice, a success not a
little due to his friendship with the lord chancellor.

'Corporal Full-Bottom,' said the captain again, mastering a
grin, 'you have been charged with being drunk and disorderly
on Sunday, the tenth of July, on this year, and with uttering
obscene and blasphemous words on the Lord's Day. For these
offences you have been sentenced to receive twenty lashes and
by the express orders of the commandant, in accordance with
the discretion given him in the King's Regulations, you will
receive this punishment with your breeches lowered, on your
buttocks.'

'Yessur,' whispered the lord chancellor.

The captain rose. Hooking his thumbs into his uniform—
his habitual gesture with his gown when he addressed the
court—he said in a parade-ground bellow, 'All ranks, atten-
shun! Witness punishment!'

In the lord chancellor's mind, a hundred soldiers, drawn

up on three sides of the square, gazed at him with pitiless and lewd eyes.

'Come on over 'ere,' said the drummer boy crisply. 'At the double and be smart about it.'

The lord chancellor obeyed, trotting to the triangle. 'Strip!' said the boy, and Corporal Full-Bottom removed all his clothing save his boots and breeches. Spreading his legs and raising his arms, he watched Tom fasten him with leather straps. Then, facing the broad grins of a hundred men, the lord chancellor felt his breeches and drawers lowered by expert fingers.

There was a long pause. This, the lord chancellor knew, was *de rigueur* in military circles, but it always worried him. Even now his thoughts began to stray, this time to the disaster of Yorktown. He was redrawing the plan of battle in spite of himself when he heard, gratefully, the captain say, 'Drummer Evans, do your duty!' and the first lash drove the mistakes of Yorktown from his mind.

It was not a very painful stroke. The captain had explained things to Tom before their very first session. With several guffaws, the Captain had explained the significance of the woolsack on which Corporal Full-Bottom would have to sit. It represented, he explained, the greatness of England, which had been founded, centuries before, on the excellence of the cloth they had spun, just as the chancellor would represent the majesty of rule under law which was the glory of the English. The woolsack, however, was a good deal harder than it looked. It would be unseemly if the lord chancellor, when seating himself on the historic cushion, should leap to his feet with a small cry of anguish. Tom, therefore, laid on lightly.

The twenty lashes delivered, Corporal Full-Bottom lay contentedly against the crossbar of the triangle. Somewhat to his surprise, he heard the drummer boy dismissed. He heard him go, the boy jingling coins in his pocket. This was most unusual, since the corporal was still tied up and his breeches still down. There was a still greater surprise when the captain, standing behind him, said, 'Lord Thurlow, I want to speak to you, and speak to you seriously.'

'But, my dear fellow,' said the lord chancellor piteously, 'at least untie me first.'

'No,' said the captain, 'I like you just as you are. This way you've got to listen to me. You never have before, you know.'

'But, Harry,' said the lord chancellor, 'you're spoiling *everything*.'

'It's you who are spoiling everything,' said Harry, 'including a splendid career. I insist you listen to me.'

'Oh, very well,' said the lord chancellor, and then added morosely, 'I shall have that dream about George Washington tonight, and I'll be fit for nothing in the morning.'

'Thurlow, do you know a boy called Beckford?'

'He's not a boy. He's a married man.'

'He's twenty, he's a boy, and married or not, he's a damned pretty one.'

'He's not my type,' protested the lord chancellor.

'This boy has asked you to ask the king to give him a peerage, and you've done so. Right or wrong, my lord?'

'I don't see why he shouldn't be a peer,' grumbled the lord chancellor. 'He's got more money than most members of the House of Lords and, God help me, he's certainly got more brains.'

'Are you aware that your precious candidate for a coronet is having an open affair with a schoolboy of fifteen?'

The lord chancellor was silent. Then he said, 'Harry, my arms are aching.'

'Were you aware of it?' Harry insisted.

'No.'

'Well, I'll tell you who is—Loughborough.'

'That boor,' said Thurlow.

'And that boor means to ruin you. He's going to tell everybody that you're a sodomite who's close friends with another sodomite whom you're foisting on the king.'

Thurlow made no comment for a long while. Then he said in a pleading voice, 'Harry, do pull up my breeches. My tail is getting chilly, and I'll catch cold.'

'I thought Tom had warmed it for you,' said Harry remorselessly.

'It's wearing off,' said Lord Thurlow in a small voice.

'Don't try and change the subject of the conversation,' said Harry. 'Loughborough is going to accuse *you*, the Lord Chancellor of England, of being a bugger. And he's going to raise such a dust that you'll have to resign. He wants to step into your shoes.'

'I know,' said Lord Thurlow. 'The scheming bastard. What shall I do, Harry? Give me some of that good advice you're always giving me.'

'And which you never take,' said Harry. 'I want you to go to the king and to say that for reasons which you think good and proper you withdraw your recommendation. Make sure everybody knows it, and make double sure you never see Beckford again.'

Even with his breeches down the lord chancellor had a keen legal mind. He grasped the implications of Harry's plan.

'But if I do that, I'll ruin Beckford. I'll be as good as accusing him of sodomy.'

'Either you ruin Beckford, or Loughborough ruins you. Who's Beckford? A monied upstart. *You* are lord chancellor.'

'I shall feel very shabby,' said Lord Thurlow.

'Make up your mind,' said Harry. 'Take your own time. I'm going to leave you tied up there until you promise you'll do as I say.'

Thurlow sighed.

'All right,' he said.

'On your word of honour?'

'On my word of honour.'

'Very well,' said Harry. 'I shall untie you. And this had better be the last of our little games till it all blows over.'

If, as the Latin tag has it, sadness follows coitus, with His Royal Highness the Prince of Wales the depression lasted very briefly. As soon as he had put back his nightcap (which he always took off before making love, out of respect for the fair sex), he was seized by an irrepressible desire to gossip. Harriet, who knew this, was always quick to give him his cue.

Thus, lying in the great four-poster, the curtains closed on three sides and the light from the candles gently coming through the fourth, she said, as soon as the nightcap was on, 'Prinny, what's all this talk about the lord chancellor seeing the king this morning?'

'Normally,' said Prinny rapidly, 'I never say a word about what transpires in my father's cabinet. He's got his secrets, and I've got mine.'

'Oh,' said Harriet, 'if it's a secret, you mustn't tell me. Let's just go to sleep.'

'Well, *secret*,' said Prinny, 'for the *hoi polloi* of the court. But I don't see I'm bound to keep it a secret from you because, I mean, it concerns you, so you're sure to hear about it sooner or later.'

'Concerns *me*, Prinny?'

'Well, not personally, d'you know, but in your capacity as an aunt ... er ... by marriage.'

'Then, in my capacity as an aunt by marriage, tell me what went on.'

'Not *your* marriage, of course,' amended Prinny.

'How confusing you are, Prinny. But then, to be confusing is the mark of a master politician, I always think.'

'Do you?' said Prinny, beaming. 'So do I. What's that damned song they're making everybody sing nowadays? About Us,' said Prinny, and she could see by the way he pushed out his chest in his nightgown that the word did not refer to herself and her royal lover.

'You mean "God Save the King," ' she said.

'That's it,' said Prinny. 'Of all the damned lugubrious tunes! Just my father's taste. If anybody dares sing it when I'm king, I'll send him to the Tower. Where was I? Ah, yes. What does the fellah who wrote the words ask the king to do? "*Confuse* their politics." There you are, you see.'

'I think, Prinny, it's "confound their politics." '

'Same thing, me dear, same thing.'

'If you say so, Prinny, it is. There's not much about politics you don't know.'

'No, there isn't, is there?' said Prinny, punching the pillow into a more comfortable shape. 'In my position I can see both sides of every question. That's why the bastards don't like listening to me. I'm too impartial. Olympian, I suppose you might say.' He made a puffing and blowing noise with his lips that always reminded Harriet of a horse.

'Tell me, then,' she said, 'quite impartially—what the lord chancellor said to the king.'

'Quite impartially, the man made a howling arse of himself, and the king as good as said so as soon as the fool was out of the door. He withdrew his recommendation for Beckford's peerage.'

'Oh!' said Harriet in artful dismay. 'Why?'

'I don't like to tell you. It might hurt your feelings. After all, he's married to your niece.'

'Aunts have no feelings, only responsibilities. I must know all, Prinny.'

'Well, if you choose. It's about boys. They say he's a pederast.'

'How cruel of them!'

'Politics is a cruel business. Loughborough's an ambitious man. He wants to pull Thurlow down. And just see how that fool of a chancellor's fallen into his trap. By withdrawing his backing for Beckford, he's as good as admitted that his protégé is a pouf. So immediately the king concludes that Thurlow is a pouf. You can't touch pitch without being defiled.'

'I'm sure you're right,' said Harriet, in as feminine a voice as she could manage, 'but I'm only a poor woman, and I'm quite out of my depth. I mean, Beckford is *married*.'

'That's a bagatelle for a politician like Loughborough,' said the prince. 'He's spreading it around that it's a marriage of convenience to fob off public opinion.' He began making gestures with a pudgy forefinger. 'So the fact that he's married is proof he's a pederast, and *that's* proof that Thurlow is one too. *Quod erat demonstrandum*.'

'Oh, dear,' said Harriet, 'oh, dear, oh, dear.' She brushed her eye as though taking away a tear.

'Don't cry, my sweet,' said Prinny. 'Politics is all rough-and-tumble, and you must expect people to get hurt.' He coughed importantly.

'Yes, but it's Beckford's wife that's going to be hurt. My n-n-niece. Oh, Prinny, what can I do to help her?' She turned her ample form towards him and took him in appealing arms.

'Tell her to get Beckford to get her with child.' Then he

added, gruffly, 'And I will come to the christening. That'll put a spoke in Loughborough's wheels.'

'It's a splendid idea,' said Harriet, without any great enthusiasm. 'Still, looking as you do on both sides of the question, supposing....' She tailed off uncertainly.

'Supposing Beckford can't?' said Prinny.

'Yes,' whispered Harriet.

'Then his *wife* must have a child.'

Harriet pushed herself up on one arm and looked down at her lover's face.

'Prinny,' she said, 'what do you mean?'

'I mean,' said Prinny, staring back at her, 'that it's a wise child who knows his own father. It's been a saying in our royal family for generations. And when your niece has had her baby, I'll still come to the christening.'

'Oh, you ... you Machiavelli, you,' she said delightedly.

'*That* Italian commoner,' said Prinny disparagingly. 'Come, you hussy, give us a kiss.'

It may have been an idea of the British Machiavelli, or it may have been schemed by Harriet. Whatever the cause, Margaret and William received an invitation to stay at Powderham Hall, the seat of Viscount Cavendish and his wife, to say nothing of their adored son, William Courtenay. Since the invitation was given for a time when Beckford would be in London, it was probably Harriet's notion, for as the scandal grew, she kept herself minutely informed of all that went on at the Beckfords' house.

Margaret immediately consulted her, and Harriet replied in a letter, or rather a packet, for she had a very large and flowing hand. Harriet thought the idea capital. The news of Margaret's visit would be a douche of cold water on the scandalmongers. The viscount and viscountess would scarcely invite Beckford's wife to stay beneath their roof if they really believed that their own son had usurped her marriage bed. The visit would, Harriet had written on the fourth page (on and around the margin, for that was her habit), be a bore. The viscount was a hypochondriac with one foot in the grave; his wife was a chucklehead who devoted her life to spoiling the son and heir.

Margaret went to Powderham Hall and found the description very fitting. The boy, William, was something of a surprise. He was as beautiful as Beckford had tirelessly spoken of him, but he was more delicate—a slim figure, fragile hands and narrow wrists. His resemblance to Beckford was remarkable. He might well, thought Margaret, watching him at the table, have been Beckford's younger brother. He had picked up some of Beckford's mannerisms into the bargain. When attention was not paid to him, he inclined his head forward and allowed melancholy to creep into his eyes. He spoke with care like Beckford, sometimes with a flicker of irony. Margaret felt a fondness grow in her towards him. Just so, she thought, their son might be, if they ever had a son. As for that possibility, so far Beckford had dutifully slept in their bed and had even been affectionate, kissing her, admiring her hair, praising her beauty and invariably—quailing at the breach. Harriet had pointed out that boys cannot have babies; neither, reflected Margaret sadly, could virgins, except on one celebrated occasion, and that had needed a lot of abstract theology.

The viscount retired immediately after his supper, nursing his ills, and the company in the drawing room broke up early, a thunderstorm rumbling and flashing on the horizon and threatening to make the country roads difficult. Margaret went up to her bedroom, the boy Courtenay having kissed her hand with empressement when he said good-night. Her maid undressed her, and she put on a dressing gown in Oriental embroidery that Beckford had bought her. As she put it on, she felt lonely, for Beckford, apart from his one spectacular shortcoming, was an ideal husband.

She decided to busy herself by writing to Harriet. Her aunt had demanded instant news of any hint of the scandal, but there had been none at all. Beckford, she gathered, had charmed the father by telling him of Eastern cures and potions and promising to obtain them. The viscountess, noticing the resemblance between her son and Beckford, had clucked and flapped over him to her fill. Margaret, composing sentences in her head, got out her writing case and sat at a table. But the chair was hard and uncomfortable, and the table was too high. She rose, and taking writing case and the inkwell with her, she moved to a sofa. With the writing case on her knee and the inkwell on an occasional table beside her, she set about the letter.

She had finished a page when there was a tap at the door.

'Yes?' she said.

A girl's voice answered, 'It's me, ma'am, with the warming pan.'

'Come in, Matilda,' said Margaret, and bent over her new page. After a while, without looking up, she said, 'Make up the fire, Matilda. It will probably get cold when the rain comes.'

She heard sounds of coals being placed in the grate, then a voice saying, 'Will that be right, ma'am? I've put on four lumps.' The voice began in a piping treble but suddenly broke into a bass.

Startled, Margaret looked up to see William Courtenay standing by the fire, a schoolboy grin on his face.

'William!' said Margaret. 'What are you doing here?' She hastily hid the letter in the writing case.

'I've been wanting so much to talk to you ever since William told me all about you and how wonderful you are,' said the boy, his voice now in his control and in a middle register.

Margaret saw that he was a little flushed with the wine that he had drunk at supper. It made him more handsome than ever.

'Why, yes,' said Margaret. 'And I've wanted to talk to you. But, William, *here*, and at *this* time. . . .'

'I'd never get a chance to talk to you anywhere else. There's always Mother. It . . . it gets very lonely here sometimes, for me, I mean, I mean. . . .'

Margaret observed how he tilted his head and how sad he made his eyes, and her heart went out to the boy.

'Well, come and sit down,' she said, patting the sofa. The boy came quickly, moving gracefully and neatly. Beckford had often told her of the way he moved.

He sat down. Then Margaret said suddenly, 'But you're not Matilda.'

'No, ma'am,' said Courtenay, once more in a maidservant's voice. 'Beggin' yer pardon, ma'am.'

Margaret laughed.

'But what about the warming pan? Matilda will bring it and find you here.'

'No, she won't,' said Courtenay. 'We don't have them at Powderham. The Cavendishes are spartan. D'you know, you're even more beautiful than William says.'

'And you're even more beautiful . . . I mean good-looking,' said Margaret.

'I knew you'd let me talk to you,' said Courtenay. 'William says you're the only person in the world he can talk to.'

'Does he talk to you?'

'Sometimes. But then sometimes he just likes me to romp

about as I did when he first met me—when I was a small boy. He doesn't want me to become a man.'

Margaret laughed again. 'Yes. He's told me that.'

'But,' said Courtenay in Beckford's deliberate voice, 'I *am* a man.' He looked deeply, sadly, into her eyes.

Margaret looked down at her writing case to hide her embarrassment. She thought of Harriet and what she had told her of her amorous encounter with Courtenay. She placed the writing case carefully on the small table.

'Yes,' she said. 'I suppose you are.'

'I say,' said Courtenay, after a pause.

'Yes?'

'I say, just because I'm great friends with your husband, I hope you don't think I don't like girls.'

'*Do* you like girls?' asked Margaret.

'Oh, yes, very much. Well, not girls exactly. Fact is,' said Courtenay with a mature expression, 'I like women. Girls are silly. I like women who are older than myself.'

'I hope not very much older,' said Margaret with her mother's primness.

'Fact is,' said Courtenay with a sharp intake of breath, 'I don't like women. I like *a* woman.'

'How old is she?' said Margaret, endeavouring in her mind to work out just how old Harriet must be.

'Twenty,' said Courtenay.

Margaret raised her eyebrows in surprise but made no comment.

'Well,' said Courtenay, a little impatiently, 'aren't you going to ask me who she is?'

'Certainly not. In matters of the heart a gentleman must never name a lady's name.'

'Oh!' said Courtenay. 'Nobody told me that.' He stuck out

his lower lip in a frustrated manner. After a moment, his face brightened again.

'Tell me, what's it like being married to William?'

'I am very happy,' said Margaret.

' 'Course you are, but I mean, well, William doesn't make love to you, does he? I mean, he told me he doesn't.'

Margaret coloured. 'Aren't you being very bold?' she said.

'Your Aunt Harriet says that when Prinny becomes king, everybody will be much more bold. It'll be the fashion.'

'And I suppose Aunt Harriet has been giving you lessons in being bold,' said Margaret.

'Ever so bold,' said Courtenay, impertinently, his eyes dancing. 'Harriet says I'm going to make somebody a good husband.'

'You are a froward boy,' said Margaret.

'I'm not a boy any more, but I *am* froward.'

They listened for a moment to the thunder of approaching storm and then to the rain. Courtenay edged himself nearer.

'I hope you're frightened of storms,' he said.

'Why?'

'Because if you were, I could put my arms around you and protect you.'

'Master William,' said Margaret, leaning away from him. 'I adore thunder and lightning. It is my favourite weather.'

The thunder rumbled loudly, and under its cover Courtenay said, 'I adore *you*.'

'William!' said Margaret.

'I want to kiss you,' said the boy urgently. 'I'm *going* to kiss you.' He leaned towards her. His resemblance to Beckford was, thought Margaret, quite extraordinary. She struggled to keep her head, but as the boy took her in his arms, the resemblance quite confused her, and instead of keeping her head, she lost it.

Courtenay kissed her, a young and passionate kiss. He drew back.

'You've never been kissed properly, have you?' He said. 'Beckford's no damned good at kissing.'

'You are a wicked and depraved boy,' said Margaret but without undue reprobation.

'Man,' corrected Courtenay. 'Wicked and depraved *man*.'

Someone tapped at the door. Margaret got up in alarm, and Courtenay also got to his feet.

'Who is it?' said Margaret.

'Matilda,' said a voice. 'Are you all right, ma'am?'

'Perfectly all right.'

'Well, what with the storm and all,' said Matilda through the closed door, 'and I know how frightened you are of thunder, I wondered if you'd like me to hold your hand as I always do.'

'No, Matilda,' said Margaret firmly. 'I am quite all right. In fact, I was asleep until you woke me up.'

'Sorry, ma'am, I'm sure,' said Matilda. 'Good-night, ma'am.'

'Good-night, Matilda. Sleep well.'

Margaret turned to Courtenay. His smile, she saw, was enchanting. How complicated it was, she thought, that he should know that her husband was not good at kissing. But, she decided, the boy was right.

'Now you must go,' she said, but there was, at that moment, a particularly loud clap of thunder.

'Well,' said Courtenay, mimicking Matilda, 'what with the storm an' all, I wondered if you'd like me to hold your hand.'

Margaret laughed. Courtenay laughed. He took her hand.

'Only while the storm lasts,' said Margaret. 'For I do confess, I'm very frightened of storms. But you must not kiss me again.'

'Of course not,' said Courtenay, and did so.

Margaret's wifely virtue did not fall that night; the thunder-storm was very brief. But the next day Courtenay took her for a ride in his phaeton, and he handled the horses with so much dash and brio and drove them at such a spanking pace that Margaret had to cling to him when they went around corners. But he was not coarse like other young men who drove phaetons. When they rested on some grassy bank, he talked to her so gently she felt she was talking to a sister, which only added to her complications.

Still, the days passed, and she continued to be in his company. She felt that it helped her understand her husband better. She was no longer puzzled by Beckford's passion for the boy. She felt it herself.

One night she had gone to bed and taken with her a letter from Beckford to reread. It was rather dull. Her husband was in some legal tangle over his father's will, for Beckford's father had left many bastards behind him—six, if she remembered what Beckford had once said—whom he had always regarded with the greatest affection and unconcealed pride. They were suing for more money than William had seen fit to give them, and he would have to stay in London for some weeks more, since the thing was being taken to court.

Feeling very lonely, she tucked the letter under her pillow. As she did so, Courtenay came into the room. He walked without a word to the fire and warmed his hands. He was in his shirt and breeches, without his jacket. Margaret thought how much he looked like Beckford, when her husband was preparing for bed. But Margaret's virginal eyes were sharp to notice one difference. Beckford's breeches never outlined so rigid a member. Margaret had dutifully followed all of Harriet's womanly advice when in bed with her husband but with very moderate success. Here, as she studied Courtenay in the firelight, the thing was done, without her lifting a finger.

'You look like William,' she said in a small voice.

Courtenay walked over to her bed. He stood beside it, proudly looking down at himself.

'Do I?' he said.

'No,' said Margaret. 'I wish you did. I mean I wish *he* did. Oh, mercy me, it is all so confusing.'

'Not really,' said Courtenay, getting into bed beside her. He kissed her, and her thoughts were much clearer.

When Courtenay had unbuttoned his breeches and put Margaret's hand inside them, she loyally tried to think the breeches were her husband's, but the imaginative effort being too great, she gave up trying.

The Prince of Wales lay back on his pillow, sighed, but, to Harriet's surprise as she lay beside him, was silent.

'What's the latest from the court, Prinny?' she said encouragingly.

'Nothing,' said Prinny grumpily.

'Really nothing?'

'Not a damned thing. You got anything?'

Harriet, who was feeling sleepy (Prinny made vigorous love, in no very refined manner), pulled herself together. Prinny must gossip after a debauch, she told herself, or he would wake up next morning in the blackest of moods.

'Yes, I have, Prinny,' she said, sitting up in the bed. 'Beckford's boy has seduced Beckford's wife.'

Prinny too sat up. 'So she's been poked at last, has she? Stout fella! How did she take it?'

'She's glowing. I've never seen my niece happier.'

'It's always the way,' said Prinny, punching up his pillow

contentedly. 'It's the virgins who always have the fishy look. How many times did he do it?'

'They were alone for three whole weeks,' said Harriet.

'Your niece and a schoolboy, eh?' said Prinny, and chuckled. 'Venus and Adonis, eh, what, what?'

'Venus did not succeed in seducing Adonis,' said Harriet primly.

'All right, you bloody bluestocking,' said Prinny amiably. 'How you remember all these classical stories I don't know.'

'I have a dirty mind,' said Harriet. 'What's Loughborough up to?'

'Didn't you know?' said Prinny.

'People are keeping things from me, since I'm in the family,' said Harriet. 'It's most provoking.'

'Loughborough's spreading the rumour that there's going to be a sensational divorce,' said Prinny, now comfortably at his ease. 'Seems her mother's going to put up your niece to sue for restitution of conjugal rights and go on to divorce him for sodomitic practices. The settlement should be enormous.'

'Fiddlesticks!' said Harriet.

'Everybody's saying so,' said Prinny, a little aggrieved.

'Everybody's a fool,' said Harriet. 'Margaret will never give evidence.'

'I never thought of that,' said Prinny. 'Still, Loughborough's mud will stick, and some of it will come off on Thurlow.'

'True,' said Harriet. 'I wonder if Margaret will have a baby?'

'No doubt about it,' said Prinny confidently, 'unless she jumps off a table. If this fella-me-lad pokes her often enough, she's bound to foal. Prime spunk. Fresh from the locker. Don't forget I'm coming to the christening.'

'I shall remember those poetic words you have just spoken during the ceremony. I wonder if it will be a boy or a girl.

Beckford would want a boy, I'm sure.'

'Then I hope that for the sake of the little bastard's arse, it's a girl,' said Prinny. He yawned. 'Can't keep my eyes open with matchsticks,' he said apologetically. 'Think I'll go to sleep. Must be getting old. C'mon, old girl, give us a kiss.'

The three weeks over and Beckford's case adjourned, Margaret and he were once again together in their home. Their reunion was affectionate. When they retired, Margaret watched her husband warm his hands at the fire, running her eye over his body, still youthfully slim. She pulled the bedclothes up to her chin and thought, with mixed feelings, that he had beautiful hands.

Beckford went behind a Chinese screen to get into his nightshirt and cap, a screen which he had installed for that purpose. Attired for the night, he shyly climbed into the huge bed.

'It's so long since you told me a story,' said Margaret. 'Tell me one tonight.'

Beckford kissed his wife delicately on the forehead. 'I've missed you, my dear,' he said. 'All those dreary lawyers and my father's offspring. How could he have spawned all those bastards?'

'In the usual way, I suppose,' Margaret replied dreamily. Then, recollecting herself, she said, 'A story, a story, tell me a story.'

Beckford bent his head, closed his eyes for a moment, and then said, 'I shall tell you a story that Cozens once told me.'

'That was your tutor who got sent away, wasn't it?'

'Yes,' said Beckford, a deep melancholy suffusing his eyes.

Margaret lay back on her pillow. Tutors, she thought, taught boys. Boys, she thought, will be boys, and 'boy', she thought, is such a lovely word.

'Are you listening?' said Beckford.

Margaret nodded vigorously and frowned with concentration.

'As I was saying, the Commander of the Faithful took the greatest pride in his celebrated harem. The world was scoured to supply it. There were odalisques from Algeria, pale Circassian girls from the mountains, dusky girls from Japan, Negresses with firm black breasts and tall girls from the icy wastes of Scandinavia with hair like spun gold. And all sought the Caliph's favours, and all were rewarded.'

'And the boys, too?' asked Margaret.

'Eh?' said Beckford, surprised. 'Boys?'

Margaret was covered with confusion. 'Oh, I just meant— well, you told me that in Mohammedan countries, the caliphs kept harems of boys, too, and I just thought....' She floundered and stopped.

'Why, yes, my dear, there were boys, too,' said Beckford. 'Well, at any rate, the Caliph performed prodigies in his harem, but such exercises began to tell on him. His vizier, noting the signs, advised him to consult a sage from the Himalayas who happened to be passing through Baghdad.'

'Haven't you told me that one before?' said Margaret.

'I don't think so,' said Beckford, a little nettled.

'I remember one about an Indian sage,' said Margaret. 'Haven't you got one about the Caliph's harem?'

'This is about the harem,' said Beckford. 'May I proceed?'

'All right.'

'The sage belonged to the Tantric sect. Tantrics, in practising certain austerities, obtain magical powers, which this sage readily demonstrated. He made gold coins appear from nothing; he read people's thoughts to their utter astonishment and, in one case, to their ruin, for he discovered that the captain of the Guard was fomenting a conspiracy against the Caliph, for which he was duly executed. He was even seen flying through the air over the roofs of Baghdad, thus giving rise to the legend of the Flying Carpet.

'Of course the Caliph was most anxious to learn his secrets. If he did, he could replenish his treasury, read his subject's thoughts and visit all parts of his vast empire in commodity and comfort.'

'Would it have helped him to cope with all those wives and favourites?' asked Margaret. 'You did say things were wearing him down.'

'You have put your finger in the very heart of the story,' said Beckford with considerable forbearance. 'The sage told him that all these powers came only to someone who conserved their vital fluids and, in particular, did not waste them in making love. In a word, said this sage, the Caliph must be perfectly absolutely chaste.'

'Your sage sounds like my mother,' said Margaret.

'I entirely fail to see the resemblance,' said Beckford quite sharply. 'The sage was a Hindu of the Saivite persuasion. Your mother is a Methodist.'

'Yes, of course,' said Margaret, and then rattled on in a manner which was new to Beckford. 'But you see, Mother was always saying that chastity was a great virtue, and if you practised it, like, for instance, nuns, well, you too could fly through the air.' Then, noticing Beckford's raised eyebrows, she said sheepishly, 'You had to wait till you got to heaven, of course.' And she giggled.

'May I continue the story?' said Beckford in a chilly voice, and Margaret answered, 'Please do.'

'The Caliph, after long meditation, accepted the sage's conditions. He no longer frequented his harem of women and— as you amended—boys. For seven long years he studied under the Tantric sage, and for seven long years he was absolutely chaste.'

Margaret sighed, and Beckford asked what she was sighing about.

'I'm thinking of all those poor women in the harem,' she said.

'No doubt,' said Beckford, 'they found other sources of consolation. Women usually do.'

'Yes,' said Margaret, as though to herself, 'there is that.'

Beckford gave her a long look. Margaret, catching it, said hastily, 'Do go on. Seven years, you said?'

'Seven,' said Beckford, but did not go on.

'Then ... then ...' said Margaret, 'did the Caliph fly through the air?'

'He did,' said Beckford and again fell silent. After a moment or two he said, 'Why are you smiling?'

'I was thinking he would have been much happier if he'd ignored the sage and just stuck to going by camel,' she said, and giggled once again.

'Margaret,' said Beckford, still regarding her fixedly, 'you are in no mood to listen tonight. So you tell *me* a story. I am sure you have one.'

'Me?' said Margaret, blushing. 'Ooo, no! I can't tell stories.'

'In that case, let us go to sleep,' said Beckford and blew out the candle.

But he lay for a long while awake.

Loughborough launched his campaign through a broadsheet which sold swiftly in the streets of London. It was headed *The Lord Cha********s Lady* and in doggerel verses made clear just what sort of person Thurlow had backed for a peerage.

Harriet, hastily summoned to Splendens by a note from

Margaret, found her in tears in her bedroom.

'My dear girl,' said Harriet, 'if you are going to carry on like this because of one obscene broadsheet, I don't know what you are going to do. Loughborough's got half Grub Street scribbling more of them. He even got some lines inserted in the play at Drury Lane, and the audience guffawed. Come, my dear, you must stand by your husband. We shall win in the end. After all, we've got the Prince of Wales on our side. Prinny says you must be seen in public. He's going to invite you to a ball, and he will ask you to partner him in a schottische. You'll be lame for a week, but Prinny can be very gracious when he wants to be. He's not a prince for nothing. Dry your eyes now, and be sensible.'

Margaret obeyed her aunt. She dried her tears, and when Harriet commanded, 'Blow your nose,' she blew it.

Then she said, 'You don't think I'm such a ninny as to cry over that poem, do you? Actually, I laughed. And of course I shall be seen in public with my husband, if I can. The trouble is, will he want to be seen in public with *me*? After,' she said, spacing her words, 'what's happened.'

Harriet subsided, rustling her silks, onto a chair. She snapped open her fan. She plied it vigorously, staring at her niece over its top. Then she closed it smartly.

'Margaret,' she said, 'are you going to have a baby?'

'Yes.'

'Who's the father?'

'You know perfectly well,' said Margaret. 'He tells you everything. He said so.'

'Thank God,' said Harriet fervently. 'I was afraid it was a footman. Beckfords are all much too handsome to have about the house. So it's that young scapegoat Courtenay, is it? Ah, I see it is. Good, good. He's a boy and knows his P's and Q's. Now you must leave everything to me, particularly your husband. I know exactly what to say to him.'

'He knows,' said Margaret.

'Who told him?'

'Dr. Arbuthnot.'

'What! That drunken sawbones! Did you call *him*?'

Margaret nodded.

'But, my dear girl, why didn't you send a message to me?
I could have sent down a court physician—'

Margaret interrupted her. 'I didn't think. I just felt unwell.
Arbuthnot came. Beckford invited him to take a glass, and
there you are.'

'Did he think the baby was his?'

'He can't possibly think the baby is his,' said Margaret.

'No,' said Harriet, 'he couldn't, could he? Not unless he
still believes they're found under the gooseberry bush. How
did he take it? Was he angry?'

'He just came in here and stood by that chair you're sitting
in and said, "Margaret, I'm going to tear this house
down."'

'Men who have just found out that they're a cuckold are apt
to express themselves in violent terms,' said Harriet saga-
ciously.

'That's just the point, Aunt Harriet, he wasn't violent. He
was just matter-of-fact. He *is* going to tear the house down.
He's going to build another and use the stones.'

'Did he say nothing else?'

'Yes. He asked me If I had any objection to the Gothic
taste, and when I said no, I hadn't, he said that was excellent
because he was rather partial to it. Then he left me, quite
quietly, not stamping out of the bedroom or anything. Since
then he's been drawing.'

'*Drawing*,' said Harriet, for once looking at a loss. 'Drawing what?'

'Towers,' said Margaret, and, silently this time, began to cry again.

Farquhar and Beckford sat on a rock in the morning sun. The rock projected into the lake that Beckford had made, romantically irregular in its banks and shadowed by great trees. In the distance, up on its hill, rose the tower of Fonthill Abbey. All in all, the scene greatly resembled the frontis-pieces of the books of poems about Nature which, in 1822, were much in vogue among the literati. Both men were dressed in the Byronic fashion, with a loose, flowing stock and trousers. Farquhar had obediently put on the clothes that the Turk had laid out for him that morning, not knowing if it might not be the beginnings of some other fantasy of Beckford's, like the Oriental charade they had played the day before.

But Beckford was in a pragmatic mood. He had talked of Courtenay and Margaret and the scandal.

'And that,' he said, 'is how the tower over there came to be built. Hadrian raised a monument to his boy lover because he was faithful—if there is such a thing as a faithful boy. I raised that tower because of a boy who was the very reverse.'

Farquhar studied its frets and pinnacles and turrets for a while, then said, 'It is looking very beautiful in the morning sun. But I would have thought you would have chosen the Oriental style.'

'Cozens and I, when we talked about our tower of refuge, always saw it as a vast minaret. There is one in India, and we had seen an etching of it.'

'The Kutb Minar,' said Farquhar. 'It is not very beautiful. It looks like an extinguisher for some vast candle.'

'I soon saw,' said Beckford, 'that the Oriental style would not do for Wiltshire. It needs deep shadows cast by a burning

sun and a bright blue sky behind it. It looks shabby in the
rain. Much the same can be said of the Classical style, but
these tasteless English can never be made to realize it.
Splendens, my father's house, was a Grecian eyesore till I
pulled it down. So I settled for the Gothic taste. It suited
the climate, and it suited my mood. In the beginning I called
the building I was designing Cuckold's Castle. I had, after all,
been cuckolded in a most Gothic way. My partner in a
Nameless Vice had seduced my newlywed and innocent bride.'

'How did you find out it was Courtenay?' Farquhar asked.
'Did Margaret confess?'

'Confession was quite unnecessary. She talked so much about
the boy that it was simple to guess that they had made love.
Besides, the boy fled to France and wrote me contrite letters,
without mentioning, of course, what he was contrite about.'

'I imagine you were angry with him.'

'No. You remember that Heraclitus said that you cannot
step twice into the same stream. Cozens had a version of that.
He would say that you cannot make love twice to the same
boy. Boys will be boys, but a different boy almost every day.
And you cannot predict the day when they will still look
like boys, but have become men. That is what had happened
to Courtenay. I could scarcely lay blame on him for that.
Besides, if there was any blaming to be done, Margaret took
it all to herself. She was so remorseful and guilty she
threatened to become as tedious as her Methodist mother. I
had to protest.' He smiled faintly. 'I think I was not a little
piqued. After all, *I* was the sinner. *I* was the unfaithful one.
Besides, I began to feel that there was an unspoken criticism,
not to say boast, in Margaret's tears and self-reproach. After
all, what she had done with Courtenay was a natural act.
It rather pointed up the fact that my love for the boy was not.
Besides, as the time approached, I began to look forward to

seeing Courtenay's son. After all, in eleven years he too would be eleven, as Courtenay was when I first met him.'

'But it turned out to be a daughter, I believe,' said Farquhar.

'Yes. She was not *my* daughter, of course, but I *was* her father. You no doubt find that very strange.'

'I cannot say that I do. We lovers of boys do not have sons, but we make excellent fathers.'

'Exactly,' said Beckford. 'Still, it is, as I said, strange. When Margaret was carrying the child, I fell into a deep melancholy. It was not, of course, that I had been cuckolded. I have explained that. But I had lost Courtenay. Nor could I console myself with another boy. Loughborough was on the alert for any such move, and I am sure my servants were well bribed to be on the watch. Then a most remarkable woman took me in hand. Margaret had an aunt called Harriet. She was, I may say, somewhat notorious at the time.'

'She had a connection with ... oh ...' said Farquhar, and politely stopped.

'She was one of the many mistresses of the present king when he was the Prince of Wales. She was no beauty, but she had brains, and that must have been what attracted him, for as we know to our cost, our Gracious Majesty has no brains at all. She was very close to my wife. She was delighted that her niece was with child, and naturally, she thought it was mine. She pointed out I had no women friends and that I ignored my female relations. So she undertook my education as a father. She explained the perils of childbirth, of which I was unaware. She would sit with Margaret and myself and encourage us to battle over the name the child would bear. She had long talks with me about the education my son should have—if I had a son—and she told me of the intricacies of the marriage market, should it turn out to be a daughter. I found it quite fascinating. Margaret, too, seemed to forget the child was Courtenay's, and she treated me exactly as though I were the father. I grew fonder and fonder of her as the time grew near. When she bore the child, I was as near to being in love with her as a person like myself can get. I was not even disappointed when it turned out to be a girl. Margaret was so happy with the little thing I was happy too. Harriet kept saying how like to me the baby was. This, of course, was inevitable. Courtenay could be my younger brother.'

'You appear to have been very happy,' said Farquhar.

'They were, I think,' said Beckford with deliberation, 'the only months of happiness I have had in my life. It is odd that they should be due to a woman and not a boy.'

'I doubt whether people like us look for happiness in a boy,' said Farquhar. 'A beautiful boy is an eminently desirable object, like a picture or a statue. A painting by Claude Lorrain is a desirable object. But a man who acquires it does not wreathe flowers in his hair and dance upon the lawn. He is not *happy*. He is not even content. He goes on to acquire more Claudes or perhaps drawings by the master or by his followers. Happiness is a domestic thing. Boys can never be domestic.'

Beckford agreed. 'We were exceedingly domestic. I even gave up my plan to tear down Splendens because, as Margaret said, it was "our roof". I gave up planning towers. I composed lullabies for the baby instead. I was not even troubled by Loughborough. The christening had been a grand affair. The Prince of Wales came, drunk indeed, but affable. He ogled the pretty women, clapped me on the shoulders and made a coarse joke. We had a great celebration here: fireworks and the village band. It was the last time I ever gave a grand reception. Five months later nobody would have come if I had held one. The band comes around on my birthday, but then I have paid them a stipend for years. They play my tunes.'

'I have never heard any of your music,' said Farquhar, for he saw such sadness in Beckford's face that he was alarmed. 'I suggest we stretch our legs and perhaps walk to the house, where, if you will be so kind, you could play me some of your compositions.'

Beckford brightened immediately. 'How kind of you to ask,' he said, getting to his feet. Together, they walked through the moss-grown paths to the Abbey, and once there, Beckford played on the clavichord. His compositions were not of great consequence, but as Farquhar had no ear for music at all, it did not matter. He was happy to have dispelled some of the gloom that had begun to weigh on his host.

Beckford closed the clavichord. 'I really think Loughborough would have been defeated. The broadsheets were not catching on as well as he expected. They depend on news for their popularity, and the hanging of some highwayman or another replaced the guffaws at me. Then Loughborough had a stroke of luck. Courtenay's tutor came out with the story that he had seen the boy and me together in a room through a keyhole. The story, as it spread, varied. One version was that I was seen sodomizing the boy; the other was that I beat the boy because he wouldn't let me do it. His mother and father heard it, and hell broke loose in Powderham. The father was obviously a dying man, and the Cavendish clan were horrified that Courtenay would come into the peerage with the scandal hanging over him. They wanted to have me tried and hanged,' said Beckford with a slow smile, 'for attempted sodomy. The Cavendish clan were backing the story that the boy had refused. The thing was very bad. Margaret was magnificent: she went everywhere; she denied everything. But even she, at last, said the only thing to do was to go abroad until the scandal had blown over. So we went.'

Beckford got up and went to a row of bookcases. He took out a volume and put it back.

'We took a boat for Lisbon, where I had friends, and then we went to Lausanne. People were very kind. But an odious little Englishman made a tremendous scene with another because this man had received me. The man who received me was Waley. He even came to visit me. The odious little Englishman shouted at him in public that it was astonishing that any Englishman would visit a man under such an imputation as I was under. Some regard was due, he said, to the opinion of the world.'

'Why,' said Farquhar, 'was this man living abroad himself?'

'You are very worldly, Mr. Farquhar,' said Beckford, 'but you are barking up the wrong tree. The odious little man was the historian Edward Gibbon, and although he has been accused of being an atheist, he has never been suspected of being a bugger.'

'I am surprised at so learned a man being so narrow-minded,' said Farquhar with indignation. 'Surely he must have known that in his precious Roman Empire. . . .'

'No doubt he would have absolved me if I had made love to boys in a footnote and preferably in Greek,' said Beckford. 'He made Lausanne too hot to hold us. So we went to Rome. I have had my revenge. When he died, I bought up his library. Here it is. When he got to the Elysian Fields, I trust Herodotus told him I was sitting on his books. Well, be it as it may, we went to Rome and there—' He paused. 'There,' he said, 'Margaret had another child—my Susan.'

Farquhar's expression was all curiosity.

'Your Susan,' he said.

'*My* Susan,' said Beckford, 'the present Duchess of Hamilton, and if there's a bigger cold-balled bastard than her husband, the duke, I never want to meet him. But I have talked too much about myself. Let me play you some more music.'

As he sat down at the instrument, he said, 'I can see you are dying with curiosity to know what happened in Rome. But you must ask Franchi to tell you about that.'

Farquhar, consumed with curiosity, had to wait until the next day before he could talk to the Chevalier Gregorio Fellipe Franchi, but then the circumstances were admirable. He came down to breakfast to find only Franchi at table. Franchi, who was lifting cover after cover on the huge sideboard with increasing distaste, welcomed him with his usual vivacity.

'Good morning, good morning, good morning, *dear* Mr. Farquhar. Come and make a selection from this gargantuan display. Whenever I stay at Fonthill, I steel myself to face an English breakfast, but I *never* succeed, my dear, never. Ah, the English! Their climate I can stand, their smelly dogs I can stand, but their breakfasts, no!'

'Good morning, Chevalier,' said Farquhar. 'For my part, I come from Aberdeen, and I am afraid you would find breakfasts even worse there. We eat oatmeal in the form of something called porridge.'

'Oatmeal,' said Franchi, delicately wrinkling his nose. 'Beckford once told me that Dr. Johnson was very rude about it in his celebrated *Dictionary*. He defined oatmeal as a food fit for horses and ... ah ... dear me....'

'... and Scotsmen,' said Farquhar, completing the quotation with a smile. 'As for me, I learned in India that the finest breakfast is a cup of tea and a banana.'

Franchi waved a ringed hand at a bowl loaded with fruit.

'You are served, Mr. Farquhar,' he said, and, helping himself to some toast and marmalade, he went on. 'But alas, not by one of your dark-skinned ephebes. Beckford was telling me about the one you have *imported* to London. He was most enthusiastic.'

Both men sat down. 'And that reminds me,' said Franchi, munching, 'that Beckford asked me to tell you he was very sorry but he would not be here today. He has gone to Bath. That's where he is going to live, you know, when he leaves here. He'll be back tomorrow. Meantime, you'll have to make do with me. Beckford asked me to show you some of his more special treasures. I'm a *very* good guide. I've helped Beckford choose nearly everything in the Abbey.'

Peeling his banana, Farquhar said, 'You have known Mr. Beckford a long time?'

'Years,' said Franchi. 'Too many years.'

'I personally,' said Farquhar, 'have found his company fascinating. But I suppose the charm could fade.'

'Oh, *no*,' said Franchi. 'I didn't mean that. I meant too many years for me. I'm getting middle-aged. Beckford doesn't seem to change a bit. But I'm getting fat and garrulous. And I was such a pretty boy when he fell in love with me. It was a harpsichord that brought us together.

'When Barzaba had his trouble over that schoolboy and had to leave England, he came first to Portugal. I was at the Patriarchal Seminary, which didn't inseminate patriarchs in fact—Beckford's joke—but it's where you went to learn music. I played Haydn. Beckford fell head over heels in love. So did I.'

'You played Haydn, not Mozart, by any chance?' said Farquhar, with a mischievous look.

'Haydn,' said Franchi, firmly, tossing his head. 'I know just what you are alluding to. You think I may have reminded him of that swollen-headed little German curiosity. My dear, there was really nothing in all that. They were both much too young. He buttered another piece of toast with a sulky expression, ate it, drank some coffee and then said, his good humour restored, 'Well, if you've quite finished your *exotic petit déjeuner*, allow me to conduct you on my grand tour of the Abbey.'

Franchi was, indeed, an excellent guide. He drew out treasure after treasure from the cabinets, giving the provenance of each one in detail, which he could do, for often he had been Beckford's agent in buying them. He showed off the pictures on the wall, but besides these, there were dozens unhung, lying stacked against the walls of some of the smaller rooms. One he drew out and held to the light with particular care.

'A landscape by Cozens,' he said. 'Now there is somebody with whom young Beckford was really in love. He changed his life for him. That is something I can never do. Without Cozens, I don't think there would have been a Fonthill. Well, Beckford always says that an hour of looking at beautiful things is all an honest man can do; after that he begins to tell himself lies.'

'I agree,' said Farquhar.

'Then let us go up to my apartment and rest a while. I am in the northwest turret. It sounds as though it would be furnished with pikes and arquebuses, doesn't it, but in fact, I've made it very cosy. In this barn of an Abbey, one sometimes feels a great need of being cosy.'

The rooms in the turret were filled to the brim with well-cushioned furniture, pictures of an eclectic taste and soft, silken hangings.

'Well, now,' said Franchi when his guest was comfortably installed, 'is there anything else I can tell you about Fonthill or Beckford? They're the same thing, really.'

'Yes, there is, if I can impose on your patience further,' said Farquhar.

'I love talking,' said Franchi. 'Go on, ask me.'

'Mr. Beckford was telling me yesterday about his wife and their first child.'

Franchi nodded.

'Then he came to his second daughter, Susan, the Duchess of Hamilton,' he added respectfully.

Franchi nodded. '*His* daughter,' he said, stressing the pronoun.

'Yes. *His* daughter. Naturally, I was, ah, curious—I have a curious disposition—but he said I must ask you about that.'

Franchi clapped his hands.

'He did? He did?' he said, amid laughter. 'Oh, naughty, naughty Barzaba! Very well, if he said I should tell you, then I shall. You see, when all the trouble started over that schoolboy—such a careless brat, I'm sure he babbled—Beckford sent for me. Oh, not to go to England, but to Rome, where he and Margaret had gone for refuge. He told everybody I was his secretary. I was fifteen, and the Italians are used to having boys made cardinals at that age, so it was all very acceptable. We all stayed as guests in the Borghese Palace—paying guests, of course, and paying through the nose, according to Beckford. But then nobody ever got anything for nothing out of the Borghese. Mean? I can't begin to describe how mean they were. I dreaded going to the piano nobile where they lived. I froze to my toes. All the heating they had were copper braziers on the floor, and they huddled over them and left you to turn into an icicle. We were on the second floor, and Beckford insisted on enormous fires. But just a moment. What was I supposed to be telling you about?'

'The Duchess of Hamilton,' said Farquhar. 'Or rather, her origins.'

'Yes, you slyboots,' said Franchi. 'Her origins. Well, when I arrived, she hadn't originated yet, not even started originating. But Beckford had had a curious conversation with his wife. On the Palatine Hill, it was, and he told me about it.'

Margaret surveyed the ruins with the cattle browsing peacefully among them, and then she said, 'Mr. Gibbon's Forum! I do declare that wretched man has quite spoiled it for me. I refuse to look at it.' She opened her parasol and held it in front of her.

'We can go to the other side of the hill, my dear. The view is magnificent, and there is nothing to remind you of Mr. Gibbon.'

'Then let us go,' she said, and they began to walk among the pines and the flowering bushes. Margaret, still angry with the thought of Gibbon, said, 'How a historian can stoop to listening to malicious gossip I never shall understand.'

'A good deal of history is malicious gossip,' said Beckford mildly, 'especially when it comes to the Caesars.'

'Well, all I know,' said Margaret firmly, 'is that I shall never, never read his book. I won't even have it in the house.'

'It is already there,' said Beckford. 'I bought one of the earliest copies.'

'Then I shall take it up with a pair of tongs and throw it out of the window.'

'Exactly what Mr. Gibbon would like to do with me,' said Beckford, laughing.

'You are too philosophical, William,' she said, but she laughed with him. She took his arm and pressed it.

Together they crossed the Palatine and on its far side came upon some immense brick arches.

Margaret looked around her.

'I suppose this was Julius Caesar's palace,' she said.

'No, my dear. Julius Caesar had no palace. He just had a house. But it might have been there. The Palatine was a very select neighbourhood.'

'Then whose palace was it?'

'Septimius Severus,' said Beckford. 'He was also a Caesar.'

Margaret said, thoughtfully, 'They all had the same name, didn't they? They were all called Caesar. Were they all of the same family?'

'Some were; others pretended to be. Septimius did not pretend. He was an African.'

'How strange,' said Margaret, 'to be ruled by an African.'

Beckford looked between the arches at the Tiber with its island. He hummed a tune and saw an arrogant little boy saying, 'Your king is a German.' Tears came to his eyes. Boyhood had been so beautiful, and it had gone for ever.

'Beckford,' said his wife, 'are you listening to me?'

'What were you saying, my dear? I was studying the view.'

'I was saying that even the Roman emperors thought that families were important. I mean, taking the same name, as you said they did. Do *you* think families are important, William?'

'Of course I do.'

'I mean real families, having sons, handing down your name. All that.'

'Yes, it is important,' said Beckford. 'Why do you ask?'

'William, do you love me?'

'Deeply, my dear.'

'Then will you do anything I ask, like princes in fairy tales?'

Beckford struck a pose. 'I plight my troth to my demoiselle,' he said, grinning.

'But, of course,' said Margaret, also striking a pose, 'I must ask you to do something impossible, mustn't I?'

'It is the custom, Highness.'

Margaret pressed his arm again. She dropped their bantering. She said, 'William, I want to have a child by you. You,' she said. Beckford looked away.

'We have tried,' said Beckford. 'You know we have tried.'

'I want it more than anything in the world.'

A minute passed before Beckford spoke again. Then he said, pointing, in the voice of a guide, 'These arches were not in the halls of the palace. They were merely the foundations. You may imagine, seeing their vastness, how much more impressive the actual—'

'Yes,' said Margaret. 'I may imagine.' She leaned her head against his shoulder, and together they watched a rowing boat move swiftly down the yellow waters of the river and shoot beneath an ancient arch.

Beckford and Franchi talked that night in the Borghese Palace. They sat on the balustrade of the great fountain in the courtyard, with its fanciful grottoes and its enormous statues of Roman goddesses standing like sentinels around it.

'I am glad to have you to talk to,' Beckford said. 'I've always needed someone to talk to.'

Franchi dabbled his fingers in the water, making waves that sparkled in the bright Roman moonlight.

'I saw you were upset and sad,' said Franchi. 'When Barzaba is sad, Franchi is sad. So I asked you what was the matter, and it doesn't seem so big a trouble as you seem to think.'

'But I want a son,' said Beckford. 'I want a son desperately.'

Franchi gave a chuckle.

'In my opinion,' said Beckford evenly, 'the Portuguese have the most naturally, effortlessly obscene minds in Europe.'

'We have,' said Franchi. 'And if you understood Portuguese better, you would know just how obscene we are. Well, then, with my filthy Portuguese mind I can't see any difficulty. You just jump into bed with Mrs. Beckford, take Mrs. Beckford in your arms, kiss Mrs. Beckford and stick it *up* Mrs. Beckford. The thing's done. I don't like her. I'm jealous of her. But I can't object to her being fucked by her own husband. After all, I am a good Catholic.'

'And I imagine your good Catholic Portuguese have no difficulty in fucking their wives and then going to bed with wicked, beautiful Portuguese boys like you. . . .'

'None whatever,' said Franchi.

'But I,' said Beckford, 'being a cold-blooded English Protestant, can't do it.'

'You do it with me,' said Franchi quite loudly.

'Hush,' said Beckford. 'Someone will hear.'

'Nobody in the palace speaks English,' said Franchi. 'But, Barzaba, dear, where's the difficulty? You're a man, my dear. And what a man! Just think of that thing you waved at me last night. Don't let the Pope see it. He'll want it for an obelisk.'

'With you, yes,' said Beckford. 'But the moment I get into bed with my wife—and I'm very fond of her—the moment I get into bed, well, to borrow your metaphor, if the Pope set it up as an obelisk, it would be a considerable danger to passersby.'

'And you do want a son?'

'Very much.'

'And so does your wife?'

'As I've told you.'

Franchi thought for a moment; then, with a shout of

laughter that echoed around the courtyard, he hit the water in the fountain with the flat of his hand.

Beckford, wiping the splashes off his coat, said, 'My dear boy, such childish pranks! This is my best coat.'

'So sorry, Barzaba, dear,' said Franchi. 'I have a plan.'

In the manner of Roman palaces, the rooms of the Borghese residence were strung out in long galleries, sometimes with no corridors, sometimes with a narrow rat-run carved out in the immensely thick walls and used only by servants. The suite which had been let to the Beckfords was made up of an entrance hall giving on to the grand staircase, an immense salon with a frescoed ceiling, a small room where a steward or personal maid might sleep to be on hand during the night and, lastly, a large bedroom with a four-poster bed of regal dimensions. In the salon and the bedroom were small fireplaces leading to huge chimneys. The chimney stacks on the roof were masterpieces of the Baroque taste in architecture. They worked perfectly when the mild, warm southerly winds blew, but a northerly or easterly wind caused them to return the smoke to the fireplaces. Since nothing could be done about this without offending the architect—and thus incurring the reputation of being an upstart family with no taste—the Borghese had learned to live without fires, making do, not very successfully, with braziers. Because of this, the bed was shrouded in heavy curtains. On the two sides used for climbing into bed, these parted in the middle, like the curtains in the theatres of the period.

On one chilly January night, shortly after Franchi's conversation with Beckford, Margaret had got into bed with a shudder and, closing the curtains, had awaited her husband. They had both given up reading or even talking in bed, since if the curtains were not closed, a blast of chill air would enter. She heard Beckford come in after finishing his book in the salon and sleepily heard him move about, undressing as usual behind his screen.

Soon he pushed his head in its nightcap between the curtains and said, 'It's damnably cold here. I think I shall go and drink a brandy in the salon to warm me up.'

Margaret, yawning, said, 'Yes, dear. Put on a warm dressing gown, won't you?'

Beckford left the room, presumably to go to the salon. But this expedition led him through Franchi's room. There Franchi, in his shirt and breeches, sat on his bed, its curtains pulled back. As Beckford entered, he leaped up.

'*Benvenuto,*' he said. 'Welcome! I thought you would cry off at the last moment.'

'I shall fail,' said Beckford mournfully. 'I shall fai—' but got no further because Franchi had flung his arms around him. He held him in a long and passionate embrace and kissed him. Then he pulled him, none too gently, to the bed. He lay beside him. He stroked Beckford's hair. He lifted his nightgown and, putting his hand beneath it, fondled him.

After a while he whispered, 'Wonderful, Barzaba! What a magnificent obelisk! I can almost feel the hieroglyphics. Now, quick, off you go!'

'But I can't leave you in the state I'm in,' Beckford complained.

'That's exactly what you must do,' said Franchi with as much command as he could muster.

'*No!*' said Beckford, clinging to Franchi.

'Yes!' said Franchi. 'No, not *that* "yes",' he added, pushing him away. 'I mean, "Yes, you must go to Margaret."'

'And you know what will happen when I leave *you* to go to her, don't you? Bless her heart, but it will, it always does.'

'But you won't leave me,' said Franchi. 'I've told you. I'll

146

be there. And, look, wearing my nankeen breeches you like so much.'

'All right,' said Beckford doubtfully.

'Then go,' said Franchi. 'Run.'

Beckford disappeared into the bedroom. Listening at the door, Franchi heard the creak of the bed as Beckford climbed into it, having first extinguished the bedside candelabra.

He waited some half minute, then, in his stocking feet, crept into the bedroom and stood beside the bed, close to the curtains. He heard Margaret say sleepily, 'Good-night, William'; then there was silence. Franchi bent his ear anxiously towards the curtains. Then he heard Margaret's voice. It was full of surprise.

'Oh!' said Margaret. 'Oh, William, my darling William!' Then, 'It is William, isn't it?'

'Of course, it's me,' said Beckford with some irritation.

There was silence again.

'How beautiful,' came Margaret's voice. 'I must kiss you. Hold me tightly.'

This command Beckford apparently did not obey, or at least, if he did, it was with one arm, for the other appeared through the curtain. The fingers of his hand were twiddling in a manner which admirably conveyed panic.

Instantly Franchi turned his back on the bed and, taking Beckford's hand, laid it delicately upon the seat of his breeches. He might (Franchi reflected) have kissed his lover's hand to reassure him, but Beckford had always lavished praise upon his buttocks, which, he maintained, were of the classical proportions of a Greek statue.

The hand was withdrawn. Franchi shivered with the chill of the room, but inside the curtains all was warmth and, to judge from Margaret's sighs, of a tropical degree. Together with his shivers, Franchi felt a twinge of jealousy. But firmly telling himself he was a good Catholic boy, he stuck to his post.

It was just as well that he did. A little later he heard an urgent whisper from Beckford, in Portuguese.

'Help! It's no good. Help!'

'What did you say, Willy?' came Margaret's voice dreamily.

'I said, "I love you," ' replied Beckford. 'It's an Italian term of endearment.'

'Say it again,' said Margaret.

'It's no good,' said Beckford again, in Portuguese, choking a little on the words, and thrust his hand once more through the curtains.

Franchi's devotion to Beckford stood the test, but at considerable cost to himself, because, in the cold room, he lowered his breeches. Endeavouring to repress his shivers, he reflected that in his endeavour to bring a new life into the world he stood to catch his own death of pneumonia. While Beckford restored himself, Franchi thought of that rhyme which (so he had learned in Rome) religious brides embroider on their nightdresses for the first night as a wife:

> *Non lo fo per piacer mio*
> *Lo fo per dar bambin a Dio*

Franchi mentally translated this into his native Portuguese ('I do not do this for my pleasure; I do it to give a baby to God'). But what with the cold—and Beckford—he could not for the life of him find the right rhyme.

But now, from the sounds of female ecstasy from behind the curtains, it was clear that his sacrifice had not been in vain. Groans and sighs mingled, then ceased. After a while, Franchi heard Beckford whisper, again in Portuguese, 'It's all right.'

Relieved, Franchi pulled up his breeches. He left the bed-room, and taking up a candlestick as he passed through his own chamber, he went into the salon and there poured himself a large goblet of warming brandy.

'So that,' said Farquhar 'is the origin of Her Grace, Susan, Duchess of Hamilton.'

'Thereabouts,' said Franchi, 'but stap me, if Beckford didn't take to the thing.'

'By "thing" I take it you mean making love to his wife?'

'Yes. Of course, he didn't roger her every night,' said Franchi. 'Beckford was never much of a pasha in that respect, even though he loves dressing up as one. But he "put to her", as the Italians say, often enough to thoroughly annoy me—'

'You, er, assisted?'

'No. He didn't need me. You see, once I got him over his fear that he couldn't do it, he quite enjoyed himself. There's a Vatican monsignore who was very partial to me, and he said it was all very common or garden and the church had known about it for centuries. But I think the monsignore was just showing off. He was always showing off. It was boring. Still, I find that froufrou of their silk soutanes when they walk quite fascinating. I'm told that in the Vatican they always walk quickly because it makes more froufrou. I don't think Beckford went as far as liking Margaret's froufrou. He doesn't like skirts. But he liked her. They went around Rome like lovers. And Beckford would insist on telling me all about it,' said Franchi, and sulked for a while.

Margaret and Beckford had been walking in the Borgo behind St. Peter's when the Pope came by in his coach. It was a great lumbering affair and went slowly to keep pace with the Swiss guards in their bright uniforms who walked beside it. On either side, Roman men and women fell to their knees and crossed themselves, as the Pope, through the rather green glass, absently dispensed his benedictions.

As the coach drew near, Beckford said, 'As the good Methodist daughter of your good Methodist mother, I suggest we slip up this alley. I don't know what your mother would say if she knew you were three yards away from the Abomination of Desolation which standeth in the holy places.'

But Margaret made no move. The coach drew level, and Margaret, with great grace, spread her skirts and dropped a curtsy. When the coach had gone, Beckford said, with much amusement, 'Don't tell me, my dear, that you are becoming a Catholic. That would never do. Loughborough would spread the story that I had forced you into conversion in order to obtain the blessed sacrament for me to celebrate the black mass, in honour of the devil.'

'Loughborough *is* the devil,' said Margaret. 'No, I am not becoming a Catholic. I had enough of religion when I was a girl. But I do want to be polite to the Pope. After all, he owns Rome, doesn't he? And, you see, William, I want to live here. With you.' She took his hand.

Together they walked through the narrow streets and under the tawny wall of the Vatican.

'You see,' said Margaret. 'Although there's all this religion —tons of it'—and she gestured at the fortifications—'nobody in Rome, no Roman, that is, takes it seriously. Not morally, I mean. When we left England, nobody would speak to us. Here everybody does. The Borghese are delighted to have you to stay, whatever the gossip.'

'At the rent I am paying, the Borghese would be happy to have me stay,' said Beckford, 'even if gossip said I not only seduced little boys but also ate them for breakfast. But I agree.

We are treated very well here. There are no significant titters and pointed fingers. Except, of course, from the visiting English. I am told that when English parents send their sons on the Grand Tour, they warn them to avoid two things—Beckford and drinking unboiled water.'

'William,' said Margaret, 'I am quite serious. I want to stay here, live here. You are so rich, William, you could buy the most beautiful palace in Rome—'

'No,' said Beckford. 'I would build one, high up in the Alban Hills, by a lake.'

'And think of the things you can put in it. They are digging up statues every day, and you could buy them at bargain prices. You could make the most famous collection in the world.'

'What would you do, my dear?'

'I'd be your wife. I love you, Beckford.'

'I love you, too.' He looked down at her. He put his arm around her waist. A passerby said, *'Bella!'* and Beckford said, 'So you are. I wonder why we are so happy?'

'Because now that you love me, I can understand how you love Courtenay and Franchi and—oh, all the other boys.'

They passed a rather dilapidated palazzo with peeling stucco but a beetling frieze, magnificent in its design and deep-cut execution. Beckford studied it for a while. Then he said, 'It is still early. Let us go back home and call for our carriage. We'll go up into the hills, and we shall choose the place where I shall build. We'll choose it together.'

'From then on,' said Franchi, 'we heard of nothing but the palace he was going to build at Ariccia. He was sketching ideas all day long. I kept the designs. As a matter of fact, I keep every scrap of paper that Beckford writes on. I'll show you.'

He opened a cupboard and took out a bundle of papers, on the top of which was a sheet saying, 'Beckford—projects for Ariccia.' He undid the string and drew out some designs, passing them to Farquhar.

'You see, it wouldn't have been a great gloomy Gothic place like this. It was all terraces and arcades. Look at the great windows and the flights of steps and the colonnades to walk in, all sunny and open to the breezes. And notice, Mr. Farquhar, there is no tower. It was the only time in his life that Beckford did not feel the need for one. It would have been a beautiful place—much more to my taste than Fonthill. Alas, Mr. Farquhar, it was never built. Not one stone laid upon another.'

Farquhar studied the designs.

'Sunny it most certainly would have been,' he said. 'But it would not have been Beckford. I cannot imagine him as sunny.'

'He was then, just for a while. That sad look had quite gone from his eyes. Then it happened. Margaret's time was getting near to have Susan. Rome is beautiful, but its doctors are so bad I think the Romans keep them to kill off the popes they get tired of. So we went to Switzerland again, but very quietly. Susan was born.'

Franchi gathered together the sketches.

'And Margaret died. It was puerperal fever, they said. Something women can get in childbirth. Beckford nearly went out of his mind with grief.'

Franchi retied the string with deliberate care.

'He kept saying, "I killed her. I killed her." He said it to everybody.'

'Husbands do when a thing like that happens,' said Farquhar.

'Yes, but the English were listening. Those odious English

who were living in Switzerland. Soon Loughborough got to hear of it. And he said that *that* was just what Beckford had done. He had killed his wife with ill-treatment—beatings, quarrels. He had killed her because he was a sodomite who hated women.'

Franchi sighed. He put away the plans.

'That's what Loughborough said, and all London believed him. No,' Franchi went on, closing the cupboard door, 'Beckford is not a sunny man. Never since Margaret died.'

Franchi took out another bundle of papers and drew out the top sheet.

'Here is what happened to Beckford, in Beckford's own words. It was written when Fonthill was rising daily and hundreds of workmen were building the wall around the property. It is a draft of a letter to one Lady Craven, whom I know nothing about. He wrote it three years after Margaret's death, and I rescued it from his wastepaper basket. It is rather a scribble. Would you prefer me to read it? Beckford has a difficult hand, but I know it better than my own.'

'Please do read it,' said Farquhar.

In a voice which carried echoes of Beckford's own, Franchi read:

' "I am extending my forests and sticking them full of hideous iron traps and spring guns that snap legs off as neatly as Pinchbeck's patent snuffers snuff candles. In the process of time, when my hills are completely blackened by fir, I shall retreat into the centre of this gloomy circle, like a spider into the midst of his web. If I am shy or savage, you must consider the baitings and worryings to which I allude, at home, abroad, in every region. You were in Turkey when the storm raged against me, and I was stabbed to the heart by the loss of Lady Margaret. And what was the balm poured into my wounds—a set of paragraphs accusing me of having occasioned her death by ill usage. Allowances could be made for former attacks, but none for this, and I will own to you that the recollection of this bleak stroke fills me with such horror and indignation that I sigh for the pestilential breath of an African serpent to destroy every Englishman who comes my way." '

Franchi's voice was shaking as he read the last words. He turned his face away.

'The letter always makes me cry,' he said. 'Poor, dear Barzaba.'

PART FIVE

Fonthill Abbey

BECKFORD returned from Bath the next afternoon. Meeting Farquhar, he said, 'Will you give me the pleasure of your company in a stroll among my trees? I have been cramped in a coach for most of two days, and I need to stretch my legs.'

Farquhar hesitated.

'My legs are Scot's legs and not Englishman's legs but I wonder if your steel traps like Pinchbeck's patent snuffer will be able to distinguish.'

Beckford laughed his loud, surprising guffaw.

'Franchi has been reading you his favourite letter. Dear boy! Although of course he is far from a boy now. How difficult it is for us to remember that, we lovers of boys. Did you, by the way, believe the letter?'

Farquhar was taken slightly aback.

'Be honest,' said Beckford.

'To be honest, then,' said Farquhar, recovering, 'not entirely.'

'Nor do I,' said Beckford. 'In any case, it is a foolish man who believes his own letters. Why should he tell the truth about himself with a pen when he never does with his tongue? The woman I wrote it to had fallen in love with me. She was very romantic. She thought I was a tragic figure, misused by the world. She read a great deal of Lord Byron, I believe.'

'So you did not set steel traps for Englishmen?'

'It was quite unnecessary. No Englishman came near me, except those I employed. And I would scarcely want to break good strong legs that I was paying for. But tell me, why did you "not entirely" believe the letter?'

'I shall tell you, Mr. Beckford. But I am being discourteous. You kindly invited me to walk with you to stretch your legs, and I am delaying you. Since there are no traps, shall we proceed?'

'By all means.'

The two men had walked for some distance among the trees before Farquhar said, 'As to the letter, Mr. Beckford, we Scotsmen pride ourselves in being logical. That is why we get on so famously with the French. Now you, sir, are the most logical man I have ever met south of the Border. Why, if you hated the English, should you have come back to live in England? You could have stayed abroad. You mentioned Byron. The noble lord liked gondoliers; logically, he went to Italy, there being few gondolas plying on our rivers. And there, I believe, he still is at this moment.'

'Why did I come back to England, Mr. Farquhar?' said Beckford, repeating the question. 'Why did you walk from Gravesend to London?'

'As I said when you first asked me that question, I wished to expiate my sense of guilt. I chose the Indian fashion.'

'Exactly. You, Mr. Farquhar, felt guilty of bringing your father to the grave. I felt guilty of doing the same to my wife. But observe, Mr. Farquhar, that other fathers with perfectly respectable sons have died of heart attacks; other wives of spotlessly virtuous husbands have died in childbirth. Yet we both felt guilty. Of what, Mr. Farquhar, of what? Beware of the declivity in the path,' he added. 'It is rather treacherous.'

Supporting each other, the two men descended the slope. When they were on level ground again, Beckford said,

'Neither you nor I really felt, when we had time to think, that we were responsible for those deaths. But we did feel guilty. Our unorthodox loves are considered sinful. Neither you nor I feel that they are. But we do find that they are deeply pleasurable. Indeed, it is so deep that we cannot do without them, try as we may.'

'That is very true,' said Farquhar.

'A schoolboy playing truant feels a similar pleasure—and he feels a similar guilt. We, Mr. Farquhar, are truants from society. If all the schoolboys played truant, there would be no school. If everybody behaved in our immoral way, there would be no society, because there would be no families. And that is the point. When Margaret said she wanted a baby, I knew what the serpent said to Eve. He did not tell her of the salacious delights of sex. He told her that she wanted to bear a child. Observe that the serpent said nothing at all to Adam. He completely ignored him. Before he bit the apple, Adam was a supreme egoist. He was perfectly content with himself. We are like Adam, Mr. Farquhar. We are content with our-selves. When we love, we love ourselves in a man or a boy—and we were all once boys. Lovers of women love something so utterly different from themselves that the contrast never ceases to beguile them, to perplex them, to infuriate them, and in the end it defeats them. People like us may try to share this mystery, as I did. The truant boy may creep back to school and, chastised, try to tell himself he likes his lessons. But bent over his book, he will be thinking of the fields, the woods, the stream and the clouds sailing in the sky.'

'Marriage indeed is a danger for such as us,' said Farquhar.

'You were never tempted?' asked Beckford.

'I was tempted worse than St. Anthony in the desert,' said Farquhar. 'The devil, you will remember, sent him alluring visions of girls and women in order that he should break his vows of chastity. When I arrived in England, still reasonably young with a fortune in my pocket, mothers with daughters of a marriageable age staged a perpetual display for me that the devil himself might have envied! I have not your gift of metaphor or your rich store of words, but I felt much as you did. I knew I was not a family man. Not that it is an easy thing in London to keep away from a marriageable woman. Invitations to balls and routs showered upon me. When I refused them, the mothers began to talk. I am not, like you, a courageous man. I feared scandal as my old pastor and master had taught me to fear the tawse. I thought of settling abroad, even of returning to India. But my affairs kept me here. I had begun buying and selling landed property, and that is not a business you can conduct at a long distance. So I decided to build my defences.'

'Ah! So you, too, took to building!' exclaimed Beckford.

'No, I have no talent in that direction,' said Farquhar. 'I envy and admire yours. My defences were more insubstantial. I studied the situation. I very soon came to your conclusion—namely, that women are a mystery. So I turned my attention to their beaux. These men, these boys, strove to attract women. Logically, if I analysed them, I would find out what would *repel* women. It was not easy. Women are extraordinarily eclectic. At first I thought that they looked for polite manners, but then I found them adoring fox-hunting louts whose horses had far better manners than they. I saw the beaux spending money, so I thought that meanness would repel. But mothers and daughters alike praised my careful Scots penny-pinching. Reasonably so, because the less I spent now, the more my future wife would have to get her hands on. Then, at a ball given by a client, it suddenly struck me how *clean* all the men were and, in particular, the eligible bachelors. Now, in India, I had noted that the Brahmins—' Farquhar stopped. 'But I

must not bore you with India. People who have been there
are apt to talk too much about it.'

'Pray continue, Mr. Farquhar,' said Beckford. Pointing, he
said, 'Let us take this little winding alley if you will be so
good.' When they had turned into it, Beckford said, 'The
Brahmins, you were saying?'

'The Brahmins have a passion for cleanliness. Their clothes
are always spotless. They bathe at least three times a day, and
sometimes seven. Women, I observed, are Brahminical when
it comes to the other sex. I do not doubt that when it is a
matter of the bed, they will go there with a husky sailor
covered in sweat, but that is temporary. When it comes to
a husband, they like him to be as neat and clean as a new
pin. Well, Mr. Beckford, that piece of logical deduction did
the trick. I went to a tea party given by the most dangerous
of mothers, and I had not touched soap or water for fifteen
days, or brushed my clothes or polished my shoes. The
wrinkles in my stockings were a masterpiece of rococo. I was
not asked again. Soon I was not asked anywhere. The Emperor Vespasian once said that money had no smell. But *I*
had,' said Farquhar, rubbing his hands and grinning.

'And that was your defence?' said Beckford. 'We turn
sharply left here. Pray watch your feet. The tree roots are
treacherous.'

'Yes, it was my defence,' said Farquhar, looking at the
ground and treading carefully. 'When your servant gave me
that delightful ablution, I had not taken a bath for years.
But then I knew that at Fonthill Abbey I was most unlikely
to find mothers with marriageable daughters.'

'Here we are,' said Beckford. 'Look up, Mr. Farquhar, look
at *my* defence.'

Farquhar looked up, tilted back his head, and drew in a
deep breath. The path, seemingly so natural, had been cun-

ningly devised so that it obscured all view of the Abbey until its very end. Then the tower rose up not a hundred feet away, so close that by a trick of perspective, it seemed to be falling on the spectator.

'I am awed,' said Farquhar. 'Your devices are enchanting. First the Oriental masquerade to get me to take a bath'— at which Beckford interrupted him with a loud and appreciative bellow of laughter—'and now this little path leading to this overwhelming vision of your tower. Or, perhaps you would rather say, yours and Mr. Cozens' tower.'

'You are a most understanding man,' said Beckford. 'Yes. It is my tower, but its "onlie begetter" is really Cozens. When, after Margaret had died, I saw that I was alone and would always be cut off from others, however many I held in my arms, I saw that Cozens had been right. We must build our towers, climb them and survey mankind from there. St. Anthony had his cave, St. Simeon Stylites his pillar, Beckford his tower. We all withdraw from the world, but in the end the world flocks to see us, as it did when I opened the doors for the Private View. I have often thought that when people gathered around his column to look at Stylites, many might have thought him mad, but all must have had an uneasiness when they thought of the sovereign contempt in which he so clearly held them.'

'You have created a masterpiece,' said Farquhar, running his eyes over the array of windows, the intermediate spires, the roundels, the finials and the battlements on top. 'What a pleasure it must have been for you, designing, building, watching it grow. I see you poring over the plans with your architect, with the stonemasons, the stone carvers standing respectfully around you, and you and the architect point and explain. It is a truly Romantic picture, exquisitely medieval. Who was your architect, by the way?'

'A man called Wyatt,' said Beckford, speaking unusually forcefully, 'and if wenching, whoring, gorging and being too dead drunk for days to do any work is exquisitely medieval —and I don't say it wasn't—then Wyatt, goddam his bleary eyes, was as medieval as the gargoyles on Notre Dame Cathedral. Only uglier,' Beckford added, as an after-thought.

Beckford had been stung by Farquhar's medieval picture of him with his architect and masons. It was very near to his own fantasy when he decided to build and so very far from what had happened.

There had been no doubt in Beckford's mind about the site of his tower. It must commemorate the two deep loves of his life. It must be built exactly on the place where he and Cozens had built their models out of casually piled stones. Further, it must be surrounded by the walks, the views, the countryside at large where he and Margaret had walked or driven. No foreign place would do. Fonthill was to be a retreat, but also a shrine.

The choice posed a problem, and that was the English. Beckford was now shunned by everybody. The London world was alert for a new scandal, and should one break, Beckford well knew his fate, dreaming of it (as he had told Farquhar) often in the night.

Thus, if Fonthill were to be his defence against the world, it must also have its sally port, some secret way by which he could flee if the besiegers should show signs of breaking down the entrance door. This, with considerable thought and trouble, he devised. Lyme Regis was in easy reach of Fonthill, and there, among the fishermen, the sailors and, above all, the smugglers, Beckford made himself agreeable by spending money and by being, like most of the inhabitants, a person frowned on by the law. He bought himself a fast sloop and engaged a crew who were expert in dodging the revenue runners. These he promised permanent employ. On the other side of the English Channel, a cove much used by the smugglers was also brought into the scheme by largesse. He secured that it would always be open to his sloop, whatever the chances and changes in the relations between France and England.

His escape, should it be necessary, made safe, he next turned his attention to London, from which the attack would come. Here again he was free with his money, gathering to his cause Grub Street scribblers, pimps, delators and such who would be sure to inform him in good time of any catastrophe that loomed. If Loughborough struck, Beckford would be away from under the blow before ever it descended.

There was still some risk, he knew, but it was not enough to make him change the site or build abroad. After all, there were English everywhere on the Continent, and there would always be some Mr. Gibbon or other.

He now turned his attention to finding an architect, and here he was in difficulties. Normally it would have been a matter of moving in society for a season and talking to other men who were building, of which in England there were scores, each with his favourite architect. Beckford could not do this. Since Margaret's death, no one would receive him. The only people that he saw were the agents who managed his estates in Jamaica and the lawyers who helped him fight the unending demands of his father's bastards. These knew nothing of architects.

Beckford, left to his own devices, recalled that in the days before he became a pariah, a certain Wyatt was spoken of as being the only man in England who understood the Gothic style. Beckford, always lively in his imagination, could not help forming a mental picture of this man. He would be lean, tall, sensitive, a little solemn, fond of organ music, perhaps, and detached in his manner from always staring up at vaults. Beckford wrote to him through his agents, who found his address.

Weeks went by with no reply. Beckford wrote again, more urgently, then, a month later, a peremptory letter threatening to withdraw his commission. A reply, hastily scribbled, came back with promptitude. Wyatt would present himself at Fonthill, and he named the day.

Beckford stood on the steps to welcome him, to do honour to the arts. The coach door was opened, and as un-Gothic a figure as could be imagined rolled out. Wyatt was round where he should have been pointed, and as for loving organ music, he looked more like a man who revelled in the sound of the hunting horn. His moonface was a brick red, and his nose a more pronounced scarlet. He walked unsteadily up the steps, like a man who had been drinking, and as he shook Beckford's hand, his breath told Beckford unmistakably that he had.

For an hour afterwards Beckford, who had prepared several rather trenchant things to say about aesthetics, was forced to listen to a catalogue of Wyatt's noble patrons, a survey of how much they had paid him and their shortcomings as employers. Beckford was relieved when dinner was announced.

The only other guest was Franchi, but a sumptuous meal had been arranged. As was the custom, for each section of the feast, several alternative dishes had been arranged. There were five soups, many entremets, then beef, mutton, pheasant, pork and venison. These were not all normally expected to be eaten by any one person. But Wyatt drank four soups, demolished the beef, went on to the pork, seriously damaged a pheasant and looked greedily at the venison. His consumption of wine matched his appetite. Beckford, who had promised himself table talk about Chartres and Rheims, to say nothing of the interlacing arches on Mohammedan mosques, had to sit through the meal in what would have been silence if it had not been for the noises that Wyatt made when he ate and drank. With the port, he made salacious inquiries of young Franchi of the girls in the neighbourhood, from which Franchi took refuge by dropping into Portuguese.

Beckford expected him to slide under the table any minute, but quite suddenly he said, 'To work; after all, you are paying me ten pounds a day for this visit, and you will want something for your money.'

They went into the drawing room, and there, on a marble table, Beckford had laid out his sketches. Clutching a large glass of brandy, Wyatt studied them intently. He showed no sign whatever of being drunk.

'I see you understand the Gothic taste, Mr. Beckford,' he said at last.

'I'm afraid I am a poor draughtsman,' said Beckford.

'Good enough to convey your ideas. Which are good, good.'

'Then you could build such a building?'

'Undoubtedly.'

'How long would it take?'

'About two hundred years,' said Wyatt, and drank off his glass.

'I would want it to be built quicker than that,' said Beckford.

'So did the bishops when they ordered their cathedrals. But they had to wait. You cannot hurry stonemasons.'

He sat on a couch which dented deeply with his weight.

'How much are you prepared to spend on this Abbey, Mr. Beckford?'

'As much as you ask, Mr. Wyatt. I am a very rich man.'

'So I have been told.'

'And even with my money, I cannot live two hundred years.'

Wyatt's two small eyes looked at Beckford keenly.

'These are modern times, Mr. Beckford.'

'Unfortunately, Mr. Wyatt.'

Wyatt waved a hand.

'Oh, I agree, I agree. A tasteless age, Mr. Beckford, save for a few shining lights in the darkness such as you. But this is also the age of science, Mr. Beckford, science, the handmaid of art. You have heard, perchance, of the Royal Institution?'

'I have heard the name.'

'An admirable new foundation, Mr. Beckford. Every week there is announced some new and astonishing advance. They are unlikely to be able to find you an elixir which will let you live two centuries, but with the aid of science, sir, I can put up your Abbey in five years.'

Beckford rose excitedly. He filled Wyatt's glass.

'You see, we no longer have need of stonemasons, Mr. Beckford. A few, yes, for corbels and crockets. But for the main structure, I, Mr. Beckford, have devised a system of building which dispenses with stone. Cement, Mr. Beckford, wood, Mr. Beckford: good British oak and good British cement from our historic chalk. And for the decorations, stucco, the stuff even the Romans used for imitating stone and marble. Put your trust in science and, with all becoming modesty, on *me*, Mr. Beckford, and you shall have your Abbey, raised as though by a magician's wand.'

'But will it last?' asked Beckford, most anxious to be told, like Wyatt's other clients, that it would.

'For centuries,' said Wyatt, with decision. 'I revere the past, Mr. Beckford, but I am a modern architect, and a modern architect must build with modern materials. Science,' he said magniloquently, 'marries antiquity, and you have your Abbey.'

'And you, sir,' said Beckford fervently, 'have my commission to build it.'

Wyatt got to his feet with alacrity. The two men solemnly shook hands.

Franchi rose too, and in a stage whisper such as boys use, said, 'But, Beckford, ask him how much it will *cost*.'

Wyatt instantly raised his glass.

'A toast. To science.'

Beckford drank.

'To antiquity!' he said. Both drank again. Wyatt, after one sudden lurch, collapsed heavily back onto the sofa. He swayed on his buttocks for a while, then stopped, staring glassily ahead. Two great tears formed in the corners of his eyes and then rolled down his cheeks.

'My dear Mr. Wyatt,' said Beckford, much concerned, 'is there anything wrong?'

'Isser building,' said Wyatt, in a slurred manner. More tears followed.

'These artists, they are so emotional,' whispered Beckford to Franchi in Portuguese. 'Give the poor fellow some more brandy. He is suffering the pangs of creation.'

'Pangs, my arse,' said Franchi in the same language. 'He's drunk. If you give him any more, he'll fall on the floor.'

'Zer building,' repeated Wyatt, slurring more than ever. 'Another damned building.'

'My dear sir,' said Beckford. 'I don't understand.'

' 'Course you don't unnerstand,' said Wyatt. 'You're not an arch-arch-architect. Me? I *am*.'

'A most distinguished one,' said Beckford.

'A mos' distinguished sodding cook,' said Wyatt.

'That too?' said Beckford with forced lightness. 'I did not know that was your hobby.'

Wyatt took out a handkerchief, blew his nose, and dried

his eyes. He then pointed an accusing finger at Beckford.

'Who ordered that meal? You?'

Beckford, on the way to being sorely offended, said, 'Certainly not. I leave such things to my head cook. I am sorry if....'

'Ah!' said Wyatt, nodding his head several times. 'You see? You jus' say to the cook, "I want a bleedin' banquet for a guest tonight. That'll be all, Jenkins!"'

'His name is De la Tour,' said Beckford stiffly. 'He is French.'

'Do you go down into the kitchen and lift the lids, taste the soup, nag about the joint and stick a finger in the custard?'

'If I did, De la Tour would pack his valise and go back to Paris,' said Beckford.

'There you are, you see,' said Wyatt, smacking his knee triumphantly.

'Now me,' he said, a lachrymose note coming into his voice, 'I'm an architect. Damn good one. Know my job. What happens? They call me in. "Build me a country seat, a town house, et cetera et cetera." Do they leave it to me? You bet your breeches they don't. It must be in this style or that style, or it must be like Lord Turd's mansion, only bigger. Then the wife wants this, Mother must have something else. Auntie Pot doesn't like it, and she's got such good taste, everybody says so, so tear the whole goddamned thing up and begin again. It's a dog's life. Can I have some more brandy? Drown me sorrows.'

'By all means,' said Beckford, and since Franchi made no move, he poured it himself. As he watched Wyatt drain it down, he said, 'I can assure you, Mr. Wyatt, that in building the Abbey you will have a perfectly free hand. I shall not lift the lids or poke my finger in the custard.' Even as he said it, he reflected what a good description it was of what he would most certainly do. He sought words to make some reservation on his promise, but he was saved the trouble, for, as Franchi had predicted, Wyatt slumped off the couch and lay full length on the floor.

Franchi called two footmen, who very respectfully carried Wyatt up to his room.

When he had gone, Beckford said in a worried way, 'I wonder if he always drinks like that?'

'He does,' said Franchi. 'Or so I've heard.'

'I foresee trouble,' said Beckford.

'I foresee him falling off a scaffold and breaking his neck,' said Franchi, not without boyish relish.

'Oh, no!' said Beckford. 'I do hope not. He is the only man in England who really understands how to build in the Gothic style.'

Franchi sighed wearily.

'Well, let's hope the Abbey stands up better than its architect,' he said. 'I think I'll go to bed.'

'So shall I,' said Beckford. 'I trust I shall be able to get some sleep. It is all most disturbing.'

About three o'clock in the morning, Beckford was awakened by screams, apparently a woman's, coming from the servants' wing. Hastily pulling on a dressing gown, he ran down the corridor to where the noise was coming from. Turning the corner into the Eastern Wing, he met Franchi, also in a dressing gown.

'What is it?' said Franchi, much alarmed.

Beckford shook his head. 'Which room did it come from?'

But this question was soon answered. Wyatt came tumbling out of a door which was slammed behind him. He held a handkerchief to his face. Seeing Beckford and Franchi, he drew himself up and, steadying himself with a hand on the wainscoting, he said, with dignity, 'Unable to sleep from thinking about your admirable project, Mr. Beckford, I arose to take a turn or two about the house. But I lost my way and found myself in a young lady's room, one, I take it, of your domestics. It seems that the builder of the house had the deplorable habit of adding wings without considering the proper symmetry of the plan. The result is most confusing. I bid you good-night.'

The next morning, when Beckford met Franchi in the terrace, he said, 'It was the nursemaid. She has given her notice; apparently he leaped upon her. The word is hers. "Lep' like a ravenin' beast" is her exact phrase.'

'I suppose you paid her well.'

'Handsomely. She was not mollified; in fact, she was quite cutting. As she left she said, "And to think that my poor old father said, 'Well, at least you'll be safe from that sort of thing in Mr. Beckford's house.'"'

'The bitch!' said Franchi with a shout of laughter.

'All the same,' said Beckford. 'What about Susan and Margaret? I shall find someone to bring them up. The arrangement has the great advantage that I shall not have to dandle them to keep up appearances with the nursery staff. I find that it leaves me with quite unmentionable smells.'

'Yes,' said Franchi sympathetically, 'you have to be broken in to it when you're a boy. It's the advantage of being brought up in a large family. But still, Barzaba, dear, Susan is your own daughter.'

'Ours,' said Beckford, with a grin.

Yet in spite of Wyatt's vagaries, Fonthill continued to rise. Science, it is true, was an unreliable companion to art. Parts of the tower fell down twice during the building, and the lower half had laboriously to be rebuilt in stone. Nobody came to visit Beckford at first because of his scandalous reputation, but later because he issued no invitations. Nevertheless, the fame of Fonthill steadily grew. Wyatt himself boasted of it, with an eye to increasing his own reputation and also to make his other clients jealous. Prints were published of the design, and hack artists crept into the grounds and drew pictures of the half-completed structure, for the Gothic taste was increasingly the fashion.

One such print was to be seen on the walls of Harriet's small boudoir. It was surrounded by a hundred other mementos—watercolour portraits, silhouettes in oval gold frames and some of those blue-and-white porcelain profiles done by Mr. Wedgwood that everybody said were so old-fashioned. Gold dragons crawled over the wallpaper, for China was in vogue. But Harriet regarded them with a cold eye. Sometimes, in the lonely hours, she would curl her lips and spit back at them. There were many such hours, for she was an old woman now.

Her husband—for, to many people's surprise, it transpired that she had one—her husband, poor man, had carried his royal cuckold's horns to his grave with dignity and a star or two on his breast. He had left Harriet provided for, but that was about all. Prinny's father had died, and now everybody had to listen to him when he talked politics because he was the king. Harriet, no longer needed, withdrew into private life and scribbled her memoirs daily.

Fonthill was nearing completion when, one day, as Harriet sat working on her manuscript, her maid opened the door and said, 'A gentleman to see you, m'lady.'

Harriet laid down her pen and sighed. 'How many times have I told you that real gentlemen always give their names. He is probably a dun.'

A deep, rather sad voice came from the corridor. 'This gentleman was once called the First Gentleman.'

Harriet rose as quickly as her knees would allow.

'Prinny!' she said. A portly figure motioned the maid aside and came into the room.

'Oh, Prinny!' said Harriet, with emotion, and then, recollecting herself, curtsied deeply. 'I mean, your Majesty.'

'Rise, my dear,' said the man. 'Give us a kiss, old girl.'

Harriet leaned forward over her onetime lover's quite enormous belly and gave him a peck.

'What do you think of my rig?' said the king. He turned ponderously for her to see. He was dressed in a drab coat and trousers, with a coarse shirt. 'The effect is meant to be that of a tutor,' he said. 'At any rate, I gave the buggers the slip. Nobody knows I'm here. And I did want to see you. I'd better sit down, hadn't I?' he said, doing so. 'You can't rest *your* bum till I rest mine, because I'm the monarch. Blasted nonsense!'

Harriet, his Majesty being in repose, also sat.

'Your Majesty,' she began.

'Prinny,' corrected the king.

'Prinny,' said Harriet, 'how long is it since I was as close to you as this?'

'Can't say, Harriet. Time passes. One damn day is exactly like another now. No wonder my father went mad. Wouldn't mind going mad myself except that poor brother of mine would come to the throne. He'd make a worse king than even I do. How are you, my dear?'

'Old.'

'Not to me.'

'You are very gracious,' said Harriet.

'Can't help being gracious, Harriet. It came with the oil of unction the archbishop put on my head.'

'Yes. I was watching. I was wondering what you were thinking.'

'The old fool was positively *spooning* the muck on to my hair, and I was thinking, "Steady on, you silly old fool, what do you think I am—a salad!"'

They both laughed, much in the old way. Then they looked at each other silently.

'I like your wallpaper,' said the king at last.

'Thank you. I chose it because Nash told me you were going to use it in your new Pavilion.'

'I think of you, too. Often. But I couldn't dare come and see you. Spies everywhere!'

'Caroline?'

The king nodded. His attempt to divorce the wife he had married to pay his debts caused such a scandal that Beckford's receded to the background in the public mind, just as Nash hoped his Royal Pavilion at Brighton would eclipse the rumoured glories of Wyatt's Fonthill. The times were changing, and people were in need of the change.

'Glad you approve of my taste,' said the king, grunting in an embarrassed way. 'You always stuck up for me. People say I haven't got any taste.'

'The Royal Pavilion will be the wonder of all the wide world,' said Harriet.

'You should hear the things people say about it.'

'I've heard it looks like the Taj Mahal.'

'They say,' said the king, with an aggrieved look, 'that it looks like the Taj Mahal after it's been sat on by a herd of elephants. They say it isn't English.'

'What is?' said Harriet.

'Eh?' said the king.

'I said, when it comes to architecture, what *is* English?'

'What they call the Palladian style.'

'Palladio was an Italian.'

'Stap me, so he was. Well, *Gothic*. They say Gothic is English.'

'French,' said Harriet briefly. 'And let me tell you this. The Gothic style was invented by the Arabs who put one arch over another and got a pointed one, and, your Majesty, you can inform your faithful subjects that the Arabs invented the Taj Mahal, sat on, or not, by elephants, as the case may be.'

'Good God, old girl, you astound me,' said the king. 'You always did, you know. Where d'you get all this from?'

'A man called Beckford. Do you remember him?'

'Yes. Night and day,' said the king. 'Fact is, my dear, he's the very man I came to see you about.'

Catching a shadow of disappointment passing across Harriet's face, the king, with a pang of remorse, added, 'Besides coming to see you, my dear. It's years, I said to myself this morning, it's years since I've had one of those splendid talks with—'

Harriet cut him short with a movement of her hand. 'Thank you, Prinny,' she said. 'I quite understand. What did you want to know about Beckford?'

'Well, it's Fonthill, really. I wondered if you'd seen it. Nobody else has. Nobody goes near him. Because of the boys. Boys, women, donkeys, ducks, what's it matter beside building a masterpiece? I'd give my right arm to see it. But I dare not go. More scandal.'

'You have developed a great passion for building, Prinny. I can see that.'

'I'm an old man, Harriet. I can't fuck any more, not properly, just messing about. I can't eat any more, not properly, just pecking and picking. But I can *build*. You're right. It's a passion. I feel about domes as I used to feel about women's breasts. Ah! I see you've got an etching of Fonthill.' He got up clumsily, went over to the picture and, throwing back his head, peered at it through screwed-up eyes.

'I've seen that,' he said petulantly. 'What I want to know is what it's like inside.'

'I've seen it,' said Harriet.

'Good girl! I said to myself, "If anybody has, it'll be Harriet. She snaps her fingers at respectability!"'

'Prinny, dear, retired scarlet women *adore* respectability. I'm writing my memoirs for a bookseller, and his face grows longer with every chapter. You'll be amazed at the lies I tell. Such dull ones. I went to Fonthill, but when Beckford wasn't there. A man called the Chevalier Something-or-other kindly showed me over. After all, Beckford did marry my niece, God rest her soul.'

'Well?' said the king impatiently.

Harriet pursed her lips.

'You've got something to beat there, Prinny,' she said. 'It's awesome. Great, thin arches, roofs a mile away, windows like jewels in the sun, and furniture fit for a—well, a king. But, Prinny, it's gloomy.'

'My pavilion will never be gloomy.'

'And the chevalier said it can't be heated. The food gets cold on its way from the kitchen.'

'I've put *my* kitchen slap next to the dining room.'

'And as for the tower, I got halfway up and my old legs gave way, so I had to come down again.'

The king slapped his thigh with delight.

'Just what I said when we began. Everything on the ground floor. I said. I'm too old for stairs. Poor Beckford. And he's bankrupt.'

'*Is* he?'

'Didn't you know? He spent all that money on the building thinking he was a rich man, and then one day his factors come and tell him he's broke: dead, flat broke and up to his ears in debt.'

'But he can never be broke,' said Harriet. 'We went into all that before he married Margaret. Everybody knows his father left him a million.'

The king looked at her for a moment in silence. Then he said, with something of the patient air of the tutor he was dressed to represent, "*My* father left me much more than that.'

'I daresay he did, but. . . .'

'*But*,' said the king, 'suppose my loving subjects gave me my marching orders, as they did to James Stuart. Unless I managed to steal the crown jewels, I'd be borrowing money off the Jews in no time at all. You see, my dear, Beckford was *worth* a million, but in land. And that land was in Jamaica.'

The king lowered himself back on his chair.

'Have you ever bought a pound of sugar?' he said.

'Never.'

'Neither have I. But they tell me it's never been cheaper. Bottom's fallen out of the market. People growing sugar-cane everywhere in the Caribbean. And worse than that. *Niggers*,' said the king, solemnly.

'Has there been a rebellion?'

'No need of one. Slavery's been abolished, and Beckford can't work his estates any more. The factors kept telling him so, but Beckford wouldn't listen. He was so wrapped up in building. I don't blame him. *I* won't listen. That's the way building seizes you.'

He got up. 'Well, if you see Beckford, drop him a word of sympathy from me. No, perhaps you'd better not. It'll start gossip.'

'In any case, he doesn't see anybody. He's a recluse.'

'I don't blame him. Wish I was. I've heard that one of my

predecessors in this job, Charles the Second, once received the French ambassador while he was sitting on the closestool. I used to think that disgusting. But now I understand. The bastards wouldn't even let him shit in peace. And that reminds me: I must be going. Good-bye, Harriet. That maid of yours—can you trust her? She saw you curtsy, so she'll know who I am. Will she talk?'

'She's the same maid as I had when we were together, Prinny. She never did, and she never will.'

'Yes,' said the king. 'I remember.' He gazed at Harriet's face. His old eyes softened. 'I remember,' he said quietly.

'Back to your domes, Prinny,' said Harriet. 'Back to your domes, and God go with you.'

As Fonthill Abbey grew, so did Beckford's daughters, if that word may be used of Margaret, as well as Susan. Beckford saw them rarely when they were children, and not at all during their adolescence. But when they came to marriageable age, Beckford played the part of a good father. Or at least, he tried to. He looked around for a suitable husband and let it be known there would be a suitable dowry to gladden the right young man. Beckford's fathering quite failed with Margaret. She fell in love—'vulgarly in love', as Franchi put it—with a penniless lieutenant colonel. Colonel Orde had purchased his commission and that was about all that he contributed to the defence of his Majesty's realm. Orde's contented mediocrity enraged Beckford. But after the two had eloped, he dropped his objections and, indeed, the Ordes.

He did better with Susan, his own true daughter. The young Duke of Hamilton was in need of money. His elder sister had supervised the upbringing of the two girls in her own house. A bargain was clearly on the counter; the only question was how much Beckford would put up as a dowry for a girl with a tainted name. The negotiations took a long time, the duke crying off again and again, thoroughly earning Beckford's epithet for him: he was indeed 'cold-balled.' But they were married at last, and Susan became a duchess. Susan consoled herself by keeping in touch with her sister.

They met regularly at a sewing bee for the ladies of the county, held each week at the duchess' house. Regularly Margaret stayed behind when it was over, and she and Susan talked as they had done in the nursery.

One such sewing bee had been held when news of Beckford's financial catastrophe had begun to spread through society. The ladies, sewing fast and talking faster, sat in a circle till a clock chimed.

'Five o'clock,' said Susan, and put away her needles and thread. The ladies rose and, one by one, curtsied to Her Grace and left, promising to come again. When the last had gone, Susan heaved a sigh of relief.

'I wonder why it is called a sewing bee,' she said to Margaret. 'Bees make such a soothing sound. Those women sound like demented parrots. Come and sit by the fire, Margaret.'

'In a moment. I must put these frocks away in the chest.' She held up a little girl's smock. 'I wonder if the little heathen children really enjoy putting these things on. I remember how we both used to love running about the nursery stark naked and how cross Nanny was if she caught us.'

'Leave the packing to the maid and come and talk to me. And the piccaninnies won't be heathens. They don't get frocks to cover their little bottoms till they become Christians.'

Margaret sat on the opposite side of the fireplace to her sister. She stared into the fire.

'I've got to go and see Father,' she said.

'Money?'

'Yes. We're broke.'

'Cards?'

'Um,' said Margaret, nodding. 'It's a gambling regiment. I'm not looking forward to meeting Father. The last time I asked him for money I got the Beckford glare. You remember how you used to terrify me with it when we were children? It's strange, we're so alike, but I can't do it. I've tried, but I just go cross-eyed.'

'Margaret, are you really desperate for money?'

'Aren't we always? Why?'

'Well, I just thought that this might not be a very tactful time to raise the topic with Father.'

'Why, is he having one of those scenes with the architect fellow again?'

'I don't know. Probably. But haven't you heard what everybody is saying?'

'You forget I've been stationed in Edinburgh for the last six months and all that everybody there says is "Och" and "hoots".'

'Margaret, our father has lost all his money.'

'*No!* But how?'

'I don't quite understand much about it; you must ask my husband. But it's something to do with sugar and Jamaica.'

'But I thought we Beckfords owned Jamaica.'

'Well, if we did, we've been selling bits, and what's left isn't worth anything because, well, you remember the Reverend Merrywether?'

'The missionary? Of course.'

'You remember how he said we had all been committing a terrible sin against the Holy Ghost or something because we Beckfords kept slaves.'

'Of course I do. I was terrified. I thought he was going to

excommunicate us with bell, book and candle. And when
it all ended up by his asking us to set up the sewing bee, I had
to slip out of the room. I thought I would burst with laughter.
But he told us that there weren't any slaves any more.'

'Just so, Margaret. So there's nobody to pick the sugar
bushes.'

'I think you mean "cut the cane".'

'I'm sure you're right, dear. You were always much cleverer
at geography than I was. So it's no use asking father for
money just now. Maybe when he's sold Fonthill.'

'Sell Fonthill! But that will break his heart.'

'I'm afraid it might. I'm very much afraid that it might.'

'Oh, poor Father.'

As they did when they were children and faced with bad
news, they stared silently into the fire.

'I'm sorry about the money,' said Susan. 'I mean your not
getting it.'

'Oh,' said Margaret, with an impatient gesture. 'I'm not
thinking about that. What's it matter if that stupid husband
of mine goes without a few hundred pounds? It'd stop him
gambling. I'm thinking of Father.'

'Yes. It's strange.'

'Father losing money? Someone's cheated him, I'll be bound.
His head is always so full of beautiful things, and money's
an ugly thing. So he's easy to cheat.'

'No, what I meant was that it's strange that we both love
him because we scarcely know him. A few visits. A present
or two. That's all.'

'That's why I loved him even as a little girl. We weren't
allowed to go and visit him because he was wicked.'

'How we tried to find out about that! Remember Nanny?
"Ask no questions and you'll get told no lies",' said Susan.

'We didn't have to ask questions to get told lies. They told us nothing else. That tutor, Whitelaw, whom we plagued with questions. He just said, "There are things not fit for young ladies to know. Just remember that foreign travel weakens the moral fibre." So from then on I imagined Father living in sin with impossibly beautiful whores, changing countries each month, one from Paris, the next one from Madrid in a mantilla, an odalisque from Morocco. . . .'

'I thought he smoked opium and had exquisite hallucinations,' said Susan.

'He was romantic to us. And he looked the part. His eyes full of a secret sorrow,' said Margaret. 'So much better than Mother. They never stopped telling us about Mother. She was a Good Woman, oh, such a Good Woman! Of course, I'm sorry she died after having you, but I'm sure she was a dreadful bore.'

'And when we did find out what it was all about, were you shocked? We never talked about it.'

'By "it" you mean the boys, I take it. No. Father liked boys. Well, *I* liked boys. I quite lost my head over half a dozen of them. So I knew what Father felt.'

Susan laughed, a very superior laugh. 'It's not quite as simple as that, Margaret.'

Margaret bridled. 'No, your Grace. I'm sure I'm sorry, your Grace. We Army wives are all rather simpleminded.'

'*Touché*, my dear. We wives of dukes pick up our husbands' bad manners. Yes, I suppose it is as simple as that. What I meant was that when it's a man concerned, people call it sinful.'

'Nanny called running about without a stitch on sinful. But we didn't think it was, did we?'

'No. I don't really know what I thought about father's boys. It was as though they were just a part of his collection. Yes, that's what I thought. Something you'd expect from a man with good taste like our father. I've met Franchi. He came to look at a Canaletto my husband had bought.'

'The chevalier?' asked Margaret. 'What's he like?'

'Most charming. He adores Father. He was very flattering to me. He held my hand and said, "You have Beckford's eyes. You remind me of him when we were young together."'

They were silent again, looking into the fire. Then Margaret said, 'Susan.'

'Yes, Margaret.'

'I've met Courtenay.'

'*The* Courtenay? The one all the trouble....'

'Yes. The regiment gives a grand ball once a year. He was invited. He's a peer, now, you know, and the regiment loves its lords. He asked to be introduced to me.'

'What's he like?'

'Still very handsome. A face I took to immediately. He talked very politely. He kept looking me in the eyes. I suppose he was thinking of Beckford.'

'Wasn't it rather a bold thing to do—to ask to be introduced to you?'

'He looks like a man who does bold things. In any case, it all happened a long time ago. Maybe some old women clucked. He led me out to two dances. Then he had to leave. When he came to say good-bye, he gazed at me a moment and said, "Margaret," as though he wanted to say something. But he didn't say anything. He bowed and went.'

'Courtenay,' said Susan, 'well, well, well. Margaret, stir the fire, will you? The poker's on your side.'

Margaret took the poker and did as she was asked. Then she said, 'Susan, why did he call me "Margaret"? A gentleman doesn't address a lady by her Christian name on a first meeting at a ball.'

'Perhaps ... I don't know,' said Susan. 'Perhaps it was

because you were Father's daughter. And he and Father ... perhaps he had a sort of brotherly feeling towards you.'

'My husband said he looked so like me he might have been my elder brother.'

'Did he? It's all very complicated, isn't it?'

'Yes,' said Margaret. She hit a log with the poker to make the sparks fly. Some of them caught in the soot at the back of the chimney.

'Look,' said Margaret. 'Remember what we used to call them?'

'Soldiers going to war,' said Susan. 'They were happy days, those days in the nursery.'

It was Saturday, October 5, 1822. The sale of Fonthill and its contents was fixed for the following Tuesday, and still Farquhar had not made up his mind to buy.

Beckford gave him the catalogue that Christie had drawn up and left him to himself. The catalogue had been corrected as to its dated and historical information by Beckford and, to Farquhar's amusement, was spattered with words such as ignoramus', 'muddlehead', and phrases of which 'Can Christie get *nothing* right?' was typical.

When Farquhar was in the gallery that led up to the shrine and the great oriel window, he came upon the dwarf. He had not seen him during his stay, for Beckford's servants and assistants had a habit of being invisible unless their master summoned them. The dwarf clearly meant to speak to him, and Farquhar nervously observed the huge head on the stunted body and the malignant set of the mouth.

'You remember me?' said the dwarf.

'Why, yes,' said Farquhar. 'You opened the door to the first of the visitors to the Private View. You are, if I recall correctly, the Count Pierre ... er ...'

'The Count Pierre Colas di Grailly,' said the dwarf. 'But that's a pile of balls.'

'Ah,' said Farquhar. 'One of Mr. Beckford's whimsies, I presume.'

The dwarf did not answer for a moment.

'I remember *you*,' he said. 'You looked like a tramp, but that damned tradesman Christie practically grovelled at your feet.'

'I have had a number of dealings with him over the years, always, I suspect, to Mr. Christie's advantage.'

'He's a swindler.'

'He is,' corrected Farquhar, 'an auctioneer. Like a lawyer, it is his profession to make the worse appear the better cause.'

'You like Beckford, don't you?' said the dwarf, staring up at him.

'I have rarely met a man I liked—no, admired—no, envied—'

'You *like* him,' said the dwarf crisply. 'So do we all. Are you going to let Christie swindle him?'

'I don't know what to say,' said Farquhar cautiously.

'Look. Help me to get up and sit on that table. I want to talk to you man to man.'

Farquhar lifted the dwarf as he had asked. The dwarf swung his short legs for a while and then said:

'I'm no count. I met Beckford in a circus. He was running after a tightrope walker. Boy, of course. He wanted me to put in a good word for him. I did. It didn't come to anything. It rarely does, with Beckford. But we became friends. It was something I said to him. I said, "We've got something in common. I'll never be five foot high, and you'll never escape from the boys. And neither of us likes the idea." So he took me out of the circus, and I've been with him ever since. Guess how old I am.'

'Twenty,' said Farquhar vaguely.

'Fifty-two. I dye my hair. I should have been dead years ago. I had made up my mind to kill myself because I hated the whole human race. Beckford can talk to a person without getting a crick in his neck as I do, but he agreed with me. He hated them too. So he brought me here. He saved my life. I've never done anything for him, except play cards or run a message. He never needed me to do anything. Now's my chance to save *his* life. If Fonthill goes under the hammer of that bastard, Beckford will pine away. Think of all this,' said the dwarf, waving a stubby arm, 'going to those specimens of humans who came to the Private View. It was bad enough to have the herd of them trampling through the place.'

He had a sharply pointed nose, which he now wrinkled as though the smell of them remained.

'Well, I saw Christie bowing and scraping, and I heard him call you by your name. I found out who you were and I told Beckford that you'd been here. He seemed to know you. He told me to leave the rest to him.'

'Mr. Beckford kindly offered to sell me Fonthill Abbey,' said Farquhar. 'Lock stock and barrel, for three hundred thousand pounds.'

'Why don't you buy it?'

'It is a great deal of money.'

'Not to you. Why don't you buy it and save Beckford from dying of a broken heart? You like boys, don't you?'

'Yes.'

'Well, then, gentlemen of your ilk should hang together or you'll hang separately, as the saying goes. As for me, I've no opinion in the matter. All I can have is another dwarf.'

Farquhar walked some way down the gallery, stared fixedly at the shrine, then walked back to where the dwarf was sitting.

'You are quite right. Beckford and I have much in common. But there lies the difficulty. You see, we are both collectors.'

'All the more reason ...' began the dwarf, but Farquhar held up his hand.

'You do not understand. I have numberless pictures and trinkets, more than anyone, except perhaps Christie, knows.'

'Beckford told me.'

'He did not see a quarter of it. I have two warehouses more.'

'Then the Abbey is just the right place for you. God knows this barn is big enough.'

'I greatly fear,' said Farquhar, 'that it is precisely the wrong place for me. Look around you. See with what exquisite taste Beckford has arranged his treasures! I can never do that. Beckford was born in a great house. I was born over my father's carpenter's shop. All I know is how to *hoard* beauty.'

The dwarf jumped down from the table. He seized the skirts of Farquhar's coat.

'Then it's simple, it's settled! The thing's done!' he said excitedly. 'Franchi and I will do it for you. Have you any idea of how a place like this is put in order?'

'I have just said that I have not.'

'Every piece in it, every picture, every cabinet has been moved twenty times. Every hanging has had twenty different patterns. It took a month for us to find where to put that table there. And every time he moved anything Beckford would call in Franchi and me to say if we liked the arrangement. Then he'd tell us why *he* liked it and the next day why he didn't. Buy Fonthill, Mr. Farquhar. Bring all your treasures here, and then don't give them another thought.

Franchi and I will make *your* Fonthill as famous as we have made Beckford's.'

It began to rain early on Sunday morning, and as the hours increased, the rain became torrential. Franchi sat reading in his apartment, putting down the book from time to time to listen to the thunder of the rain on the roof of the Abbey. Then he heard another sound, so unusual that he went to the door. It was Beckford's voice shouting, 'Franchi, Franchi, come quickly!'

Franchi, obeying, met Beckford in the Great Octagon. Beckford held a sheet of paper in his hand.

Franchi went up to him. 'Gracious, Barzaba,' he said. 'Whatever has happened? Never have I heard you *shouting*, Barzaba. Is something wrong? Has the roof fallen in? If it has, I'll *hit* that man Wyatt.'

Beckford recovered his composure. 'I am sorry to have disturbed you. Was I shouting? Yes, I suppose I was. No, the roof has not fallen in, but I agree with you that any of Wyatt's roofs very well might. No, Franchi. I have to go to the printer's in Salisbury. I'd like you to come with me.'

'But, Barzaba, it's Sunday. And in all this rain!'

'We shall have to knock the printer up. I know where he lives,' said Beckford. He smiled broadly.

'Barzaba!' said Franchi severely. 'You're hiding something from me. What is it? Tell me.'

'Later,' said Beckford, smiling again. 'Just now, tell the groom to get out the phaeton.'

'*Tell* me!' said Franchi, but Beckford said nothing. 'How infuriating you can be!' said Franchi. 'And I'll not go in a phaeton in this weather. We'll go—if we must—in my britska.'

In due course, the horses were harnessed and the coachman on his box. The two footmen, because of the weather, were excused. Franchi pulled down the screen with its small panes of glass and secured the apron.

'There!' he said in a motherly way. 'You'll be nice and dry, but I'm sure you'll catch a cold all the same. Why couldn't you let me take the thing to the printer's?'

'No,' said Beckford. 'This must be done by me.' He waved the sheet of paper, which he had folded in half. 'This must be printed with the finest type, set in the most just proportions. It must be a joy to look at.'

'What is it?'

'Guess.'

'You know I *hate* guessing. Oh, Barzaba, why are you being so naughty today?' Franchi peered into Beckford's face. 'Well, all I can say is you look like the cat that's just swallowed the canary.'

'Well done,' said Beckford. 'I have.' Then he burst into his loud laugh. When he had recovered he said, tapping the paper, 'This is an announcement cancelling Tuesday's auction of Fonthill.'

'Barzaba!'

'You see, there is no need of one. At ten o'clock this morning Farquhar bought the Abbey and its contents for three hundred thousand pounds. And that means, my dear, that I have recovered every penny I spent on it and put seventy thousand pounds' profit in my pocket. You do not look as pleased as I hoped.'

'Of course I'm pleased. But at this moment I can't help thinking of Mr. Christie. And all those people coming to the sale. The king's brother-in-law has positively said he's coming and—'

'I've thought about that. I shall post this notice—two or three copies of it—at the Great West Door. That means everybody will have to drive all the way through the grounds, get out of their carriages—the print must not be too big—read the notice, and *go away*!' said Beckford, shouting for the second time that day. 'Farquhar and I have selected a window from which we will have an excellent view.'

'Everybody will be furious with you,' said Franchi.

'I hope so. Perhaps it might even rain as badly as it is doing now.'

'It'll be a scandal. They'll say, "It's Beckford again!"'

'I must remember to keep the window open so I can hear.'

'Naughty Barzaba,' said Franchi, and sighed. 'At least,' he said, 'we can pay for the britska.'

Farquhar moved into Fonthill Abbey. His collection was duly arranged. Some months later the tower collapsed, the union of antiquity and science having once more proved incomplete. Farquhar was so dismayed he took to his bed, but Beckford was unruffled. He was busy building another tower in Bath.